Jack Boyz N Da Bronx

Romell Tukes

Lock Down Publications and Ca$h
Presents
Jack Boyz N Da Bronx
A Novel by *Romell Tukes*

Romell Tukes

Lock Down Publications
P.O. Box 944
Stockbridge, Ga 30281
www.lockdownpublications.com

Copyright 2021 Romell Tukes
Jack Boyz N Da Bronx

First Edition April 2021
Printed in the United States of America

Lock Down Publications
Like our page on Facebook: Lock Down Publications @
www.facebook.com/lockdownpublications.ldp
Cover design and layout by: **Dynasty Cover Me**
Book interior design by: **Shawn Walker**
Edited by: **Tamira Butler**

Stay Connected with Us!

Text **LOCKDOWN** to 22828 to stay up-to-date with new releases, sneak peaks, contests and more...

Thank you!

Submission Guideline.

Submit the first three chapters of your completed manuscript to ldpsubmissions@gmail.com, subject line: Your book's title. The manuscript must be in a .doc file and sent as an attachment. Document should be in Times New Roman, double spaced and in size 12 font. Also, provide your synopsis and full contact information. If sending multiple submissions, they must each be in a separate email.

Have a story but no way to send it electronically? You can still submit to LDP/Ca$h Presents. Send in the first three chapters, written or typed, of your completed manuscript to:

LDP: Submissions Dept
P.O. Box 944
Stockbridge, Ga 30281

DO NOT send original manuscript. Must be a duplicate.

Provide your synopsis and a cover letter containing your full contact information.

Thanks for considering LDP and Ca$h Presents.

Acknowledgements

First and foremost, all praises are due to Allah. My family and real friends, much love for staying down while I came up, facts. Thank you to all my readers. Without y'all, where would I be? Coast to coast, much luv. Yonkers, NY, we here, upstate NY, I see y'all. Shout out to everybody in the feds and state prison. Never give up, we soldiers. Shout out to Armani C and Star Brim, I see you, ma. My Bronx team, Dru from Burrside Harris and Davis, Melly, Big Fatal, Jam Roc, and the whole BX. My Brooklyn team, OG Chuck, Tim Did, Tails, and my Crown Heights goons. Shout out to Miami, ATL, Cali, Texas, Little Rock, Murda, it's all love. To all my haters, thank you.

Romell Tukes

Chapter 1

Bronx, NY

The all-black Toyota Camry was sitting on the side block watching Patterson projects closely. It was 10:30 p.m., the perfect time to catch a nigga slipping, especially when it's a ghost town and nobody was outside.

"Damn, cuz, what the fuck son doing?" Kip Loc asked his best friend, Kazzy, staring out the windows.

"I told you, Loc, have patience, you thirsty ass nigga," Kazzy Loc replied, ice grilling his childhood friend.

"You think Knight and Fatal Brim went to go see ol' boy yet?" Kip Loc asked, bopping his head to the Lil' Dork album playing in the stolen car.

"I don't know, son, but I do know it's payday," Kazzy Loc said, smiling, seeing Weebie come out the tall building with a duffle bag in his fat hands, in a rush.

Kazzy Loc was a jack boy born and raised in the Bronx in MillBrook projects with his two brothers, Knight and Lil' K, and his sister, BeBe. Growing up was hard in a single-mother home, because their father was never around. They never even saw him, none of them. Their mother's last time seeing him was when she got pregnant with Lil' Killer, aka Lil' K. Their mom never let them meet their father nor did she talk about him.

Kazzy went by the name Kazzy Loc in the streetz because he was a Rollin' 30s crip. He was medium height, had waves, brown eyes, dimples, a chipped tooth, and was a smooth nigga. At 19 years old, he had dreams of getting rich, even if he had to die trying.

He wasn't really into drug dealing, he was more of the robbing type, and his brother was the same way.

"Jackpot, let's make our move," Kazzy said, pulling down his mask over his face, jumping out the car with Kip Loc by his side.

Kazzy and Kip Loc had been friends since elementary school. Kip Loc had a gang of brothers and sisters, but his brothers, Less and Fatal Brim, were both into the streets and he was following their lead.

Kip Loc was 19 years old and an Eight-Trey crip. He was gangbanging like he was in Compton. He was short, 5'4 height, with skinny dreads, a bunch of tattoos, and he was always on bullshit. This was the life they wanted to have. It was a rush to them and the money was good. Knight put them on to the lick and they were more than happy to collect.

***

Weebie was a fat older nigga who sold weight for Glock, who was his cousin. He had Patterson projects doing numbers on crack, and he normally picked up the profit every two weeks.

He was walking to his Benz E-Class at a fast pace for a nigga who was 340 pounds, but Weebie knew niggas was always lurking. Weebie opened the back door and placed the duffle in the backseat. As soon as he closed the door, he felt a gun to the back of his head.

"Look, man, you can take it, please just leave me alone. I swear I don't know nothing, you'll never see my face again," Weebie stated, scared to death.

"Shut your bitch ass up, nigga. Grab that bag, fuck nigga," Kazzy stated, watching him open the car door and get the bag. Kip Loc snatched the bag out Weebie's hand, just in case he wanted to try something slick.

Boc, Boc, Boc, Boc...

The shots echoed through the parking lot as car alarms went off. Kip Loc had blood all over his ski mask.

"Damn, son," Kip Loc said, taking off his mask, walking to the Toyota.

"My bad, I ain't know blood was going to get on you, cuz," Kazzy said laughing, climbing in the car on his way back across with the upset Kip Loc.

***

Long Island, NY

Knight and Fatal Brim just saw two Yukon SUV trucks pass them in their Nissan Maxima parked at the end of the block in the middle of the suburbs.

"That was him. Let's try to be in and out in ten minutes, you already know what spots to hit," Knight said to Fatal Brim, who was smoking a blunt of loud, paying his best friend no mind.

Knight and Fatal Brim were two known dangerous jack boyz who would rob any nigga if he had a bag. Knight was the laid-back smart type, and Fatal Brim was a live wire.

At twenty-two, Knight robbed a lot of niggas. He was Kazzy's oldest brother. Once he finished high school, he had a chance to play basketball in college or play in the streets. He was tall at 6'3, and had dreads that hung down his back, brown skin, was chiseled, lean, and he had a mouth full of diamonds.

D Fatal Brim was raised in the streets. With a crackhead mother and his father doing life in prison, he was left to be the man of the house with four other brothers and twin sisters.

D Fatal was a Blood gang member with some rank. He did a state bid and came out worse than he went in. D Fatal Brim had so many enemies all over the Bronx from robbing niggas, he didn't know who was out to get him.

D Fatal Brim was twenty-three, six feet, tatted from his neck to feet, dark skin, and had a small scar on his face from a Blood member he was up north with.

***

The house was nice and large with a two-car garage that was left open. Both men walked through the garage into the house that belonged to a kingpin named Fats.

"I'm going upstairs," D Fatal Brim whispered in a low-pitched voice.

"Four minutes, and don't be fucking around," Knight stated, knowing how his childhood friend was.

D Fatal Brim walked upstairs to see the bedroom door cracked open and heard moans. When he peeked inside the room, he saw a slim, red-bone bad bitch with a phat pussy masturbating with her fingers. She had thick cream cumming out her small pussy slit.

"Ahhhhhhh!" she screamed when she saw the gunman outside her door.

Boc, Boc, Boc...

D Fatal Brim shot her in her upper chest, killing her.

With a couple of minutes left, he ran in the closet and pulled up the rug off the floor to see a latch. He lifted the wood latch and saw stacks of money.

"Shit..." D Fatal Brim grabbed a Gucci bag next to him and filled the bag up with money.

Once back downstairs, Knight had a garbage bag full of blue faces.

"What happened?"

"Had to smoke a bitch," D Fatal Brim said, leaving, wondering how much money they had.

Chapter 2

Mill Brook Projects, Bronx
Later that Night

"Damn, son," D Fatal Brim said, standing in a circle looking at all the money they poured in the middle of the floor from both robberies.

"That was an ill set up, you heard," Kip Loc stated, rubbing his hands together, knowing it was close to a half a million on the floor, his biggest lick so far.

Kip Loc looked around and thought about crossing everybody in the room, even his own brother, by killing everybody and leaving with the money.

"I see that look in your eyes, brotty. What you thinking about?" Kazzy asked.

"How lucky you niggas are to be family," Kip Loc stated, making everybody laugh as Knight brought out the money machine.

Knight used a local crackhead's crib in building 530 to count the money. Knight had been plotting this lick for months with the help of Parks, who was one of Fats' ex-workers he was close with.

Parks knew everything about Fats' drug operation, and he put Knight on for a small piece of the pie. Little did Parks know, Knight was a real Bronx nigga and he had no plans of giving Parks anything.

It took the crew an hour to count the money, which all together came out to 370,000 in cash, some dirty and some clean. They split the money four ways and went their separate ways. It was just a regular day in the office for all of them.

***

"Ohh, yesss, Paco, fuck me harder," Jana moaned, bent over on the hotel bed gripping the sheets, throwing her big ass back on Paco's dick as he slashed her shit.

Jana was an older woman in her forties, but her pussy was top notch and she was a freak. She took Paco's V-card, so she knew his dick game better than any bitch because she taught him how to fuck.

Paco was going deep and spreading her phat ass while he pummeled her tight, warm pussy unmercifully, making her scream. Jana arched her lower back, closing her eyes as he grabbed her big breasts while banging her from the back.

Whap!!! Whap!!!

Paco slapped her ass cheeks twice, making her come hard. With a few more prods in her creamy love box, he pulled out, feeling himself about to shoot his load.

Jana knew what time it was. She sucked the tip of his dick slowly while opening her mouth wide, forcing him as deep as it would go down her throat.

"Shittt, Jana, suck da shit, ma," Paco said, looking down at her head viciously bobbing up and down. She was deep throating him while banging the tip of his dick as deep as it would go, then coming back up sucking while massaging his balls. When he nutted, she held her position, making sure she caught everything.

Jana was one of Pop-Off's thots. Pop-Off was a local rapper who was on his way to the top, but he was still in the streetz. Jana was a pretty brown-skin woman who loved her Spanish papis, especially Paco.

"Good looking, ma. I gotta go, I'ma call you," Paco said, getting dressed in his Balenciaga sweatsuit and tan Timberlands.

"Ok, Paco, be safe," Jana said, getting dressed in her jeans and sliding on her six-inch heels. Paco left, climbing in his red and black Ford Shelby Supersnake Mustang he just got last week from a nice lick he and Black caught in Queens, NY.

At twenty-one, Paco had his shit in order. He was a jack boy with plans. Robbing was his game but getting rich was his goal. He was Dominican, handsome, had long hair, was slim and tall, with green hazel eyes, and a charming smile that got all the ladies.

Paco was raised in Washington Heights by his mother and aunt, who were from D.R. He was down with Knight and D Fatal Brim. They were all like brothers and had a strong loyalty bond.

He now lived in Webster projects with Less, they recently moved in together last month, and the two of them together were all bad. They were best friends. Less fucked with Paco harder than his own brothers. When Paco and D Fatal Brim got into a fight, Less jumped in and beat up his own brother for Paco.

**

Webster Pjs, Bronx

Less and Black were in the crib playing PlayStation 4 for money. It was a snowy day outside, so they were in the crib.

"Man, I'm done playing this shit," Black said, putting down the controller as Less finished playing *Call of Duty*.

Black was a jack boy from Mill Brook. He was twenty years old and very smart. His mom was an NYPD cop and his little brother, Blu, was in the streetz cripping heavily, riding around on dirt bikes.

"Nigga, roll out and stop bitching," Less said, focused on the game.

"Watch your fucking mouth, son," Black said, walking into the kitchen to get something to eat.

There were guns all over the crib just in case a nigga wanted to try something. This was the hangout spot for Less, Paco, Black, Knight, and D Fatal Brim. Kazzy Loc and Kip Loc had their own thing going on, not to mention they were cripping and everybody else was Blood besides Paco, who was down with a Spanish gang called Patria.

"Yo, son, you heard about that lick bro and them caught the other night?"

"Who, Knight and Kazzy?"

"Nigga, it was Knight, Kazzy, Fatal, and Kip," Less stated, mad his brothers, Kip Loc and D Fatal Brim, didn't bring him along.

"Nah, son, but Knight on his way over here with Kazzy now," Black said, warming up old Chinese food from last night.

"Let me go downstairs, because the Macks hate Kazzy Loc," Less said, stopping the game grabbing his Glock 17. Less was a Blood gang member. He was a Mack Valla and so was Black.

Less was twenty-one years old, born and raised in Mill Brook pjs. He was light skin, medium height, loud, and had braids and a small slash on his eyebrow from a crip trying to cut him on Rikers Island.

Less was in and out of jail since he was a child, just like his older brother, D Fatal Brim. Less was a hothead with a lot to learn. His brother tried to show him the game, but he would never listen. He had an ego problem.

Chapter 3

Bronx, NY

Frank Washington, aka Fats, was in the backseat of a black Bentley Bentayga SUV filled with security guards on his way to 161st near Yankee Stadium.

Fats was one of the biggest kingpins on the East Coast with a serious plug. Fats was born and raised in Brooklyn, but he called the Bronx his home.

He was forty years old, short, fat, dark skinned, with a bald head and a big beard, and he loved to wear Louis Vuitton and big-face Rolexes. He was a millionaire with a solid crew of killers. Glock was his number one capo and his youngin' he kept on a leash.

Being raised around brothers and a strong African family, Fats grew up with a mind to conquer the world. Seeing older niggas in Bed-Stuy get money and kill shit, Fats knew that's what he wanted to do.

Last week, Fats' house got robbed and someone killed his bitch. He was more upset about the little bit of money that was gone than the bitch.

Fats knew it was an inside job because only three people knew where his stash spot was in that house.

The money that was stolen was pocket change to Fats, but it was all about respect in the streets.

The three people who knew about his stash spot were people close to him. One was Glock, his cousin, Arty, who was locked up in Cali, and last but not least, Parks, his ex-worker.

Parks wanted to start his own shit and control his own drug turf, so he and Fats had a big fallout. The only reason Fats didn't kill him was because he was close to his mother, Cara.

His goon found Parks in the South Bronx and brought him to one of Fats' buildings he owned. Fats bought real estate all across the city so he could rebuild abandoned apartments and sell them or rent them out to the poor.

They got off the exit passing the Yankee's stadium, driving down a one-way street full of buildings that looked old and run down.

Once the Bentley parked, Fats and his three large guards stepped out, walking into a brick building upstairs.

***

Parks was ass naked, tied to a cross surrounded by four men taking turns giving him body shots because Fats didn't want his face badly injured until he got what he needed out of him.

"Parks, my nigga, this is how you do me after everything I did for you? Bailed you out three times, fed your children, bought you your first Benz, gave you your first Rolex watch, and I put food on your table." Fats started looking into Parks' red, puffy eyes.

"Fats, please, it's not what you think. They made me do it, son, word to life, yo!" Parks shouted as his arms were stretched out like Jesus tied to the cross.

"Crossing me was the wrong thing to do," Fats said, picking up a steel bat from the ground, swinging at Parks' ribs.

"Ahhhh Ahhhh!" Parks screamed as his ribs broke off the impact. Fats then broke his kneecaps with the bat.

"Don't cry now, bitch nigga. Now, who you used to set me up?"

"D Fatal Brim and Knight from Mill Brook and Michelle projects. They jack boys, they robbing everythang out here. Please, they made me, Fats, you have to believe me," Parks cried with tears, unable to breath properly.

"I do, young blood. Dave, handle your business," Fats said, walking towards the door. Dave was a serious killer from Yonkers. He loved killing, and Parks knew it was over.

"Dad... please!" Parks shouted, making Fats stop.

Two years ago, Fats found out Parks was his son from Cara. The two had been fucking since they were kids, but he was surprised to find out Parks was his. When he found out Parks was his son, he kept it on the low and Cara agreed.

"It's too late for that," Fats said, turning around, hearing gunshots on his way out.

***

Jerome Ave, Bronx

It was early Monday morning and the Honda Civic was parked in a small car lot across the street from a strip full of auto shops under the four train stations.

"You heard from Parks?" Knight asked.

"Nah, son phone off. He probably out of town, scared of his own shadow, you heard," D Fatal Brim said, coughing on a blunt of loud.

"We should have killed son. I hate moving with loose ends, bro. This nigga gave us a mean setup on these niggas too easily. I know he had some wicked intentions," Knight said, watching the yellow auto body shop with the gate down.

"These niggas are big time, bro. Fats and Glock are made niggas and their whole crew getting to a bag, and we need all that. I hate that bitch ass nigga," D Fatal Brim said, referring to his long-time rival, Glock.

"Man, y'all niggas beefing over bitches, I'm focused on a bag," Knight said, seeing a white Porsche 918 Spyder pull up to the yellow shop.

"There he go," D Fatal Brim said, smiling, seeing Glock's uncle Bless open his auto body shop he sold weight out of. He was walking into the shop with a Gucci bookbag.

***

Bless was Glock's uncle and a known getting money nigga who had a small crew in Motto Haven getting money for him. Glock was his plug, but he also invested his money into two auto body shops, one in the Bronx and the other in Queens.

Bless was in his back office, placing money in his safe where he already had 140,000 in cash, two guns, and three keys of pure coke.

When he was about to close the safe, he felt a hard blow to his head, knocking him on the ground. "What the fuck!" Bless shouted, about to jump up and get busy, until he saw D Fatal Brim standing there with a Draco. He knew his face from years ago when he got robbed in Cartland projects. He hadn't ever seen the dude with the platinum grill in his mouth.

"Big Bless, nice to see you see you again," D Fatal Brim stated before shooting Bless five times in his chest. When Bless's body hit the floor, D Fatal Brim took off Bless's Rolex, chain, and pinky ring. He even took his Balenciaga sneakers.

Knight took everything out the safe, throwing it into a garbage bag while D Fatal Brim admired his new watch.

They made a clean getaway before any of the other shops opened up on the strip.

Chapter 4

Pelham Park, Bronx

Yasmine was running her daily seven miles on the track of Pelham Park. She came here every morning, Monday through Friday, at 7 am. She was twenty-eight years old and a hairstylist in her own salon.

Yasmine was Puerto Rican and raised in the Castle Hill section of the Bronx. She was a bombshell standing at five-four, was thick with C-cup breasts, bronze skin, hazel eyes, long, brown, curly hair, nice full lips, no stomach and a toned body.

Exercising was her stress reliever, especially dealing with an eight-year-old son she had with a big-time drug dealer named Glock.

The two had been together since high school. She went off to college at Miami University and came back to be with him and got pregnant on the winter break.

She had on a pair of Muscle Gang Fitness Gear (MGFG) leggings and a sweater, listening to her iPod while finishing her last lap.

In the morning was the perfect time for her to exercise while Glock and her son were asleep. On her way back to the parking lot, she saw a handsome brother stretching with no shirt on next to a van and a Honda.

Yasmine tried to pay him no mind, but he had a body of a god and he was fine. The man was now walking past her red BMW 18 towards her on his way to the track.

"Good morning," the man said, ten feet away from her.

"Good morning, early birds get the worms. I haven't seen you out here before," Yasmine said, stopping to talk but really checking him out because he had her panties soaked with her wetness.

She was loyal to Glock, but she wouldn't miss the chance to flirt to see if she still had it.

"I just started coming out here," he replied, looking at her sexy smile.

"Are those real?"

"What?"

"Your shiny teeth," she said, unaware of the man behind her. D Fatal Brim put her in a chokehold until she passed out.

Paco pulled up in the van while they tossed her body in the back before pulling off. Knight hopped in the Honda, following his crew to their secret hideout across town.

***

Highbridge, Bronx

The old factory warehouse was an abandoned place Knight used for special events, such as today.

Yasmine woke up in zip ties, laying in the middle of the floor in a puddle of water.

She tried to scream, but the duct tape around her mouth muffled her cries.

"Damn, son had a nice piece," Paco said, looking at how good Yasmine looked in distress.

"Get off that creep shit, fam," D Fatal Brim said, pulling the tape off then putting his pistol in her mouth. "Bitch, if you scream, I'll kill your dumb ass now. I'ma ask you a question and you gonna answer me. Are we clear, bitch?" D Fatal Brim said as she nodded her head.

Knight and Paco just stood there and let Brim work, because ever since they were kids, he loved to be the one to steal the show.

"Where can I find Glock?"

"Lambert projects and Soundview," she stated, giving his location up with ease because she wasn't the one on the streets with enemies.

"You can do better than that, mami," Paco said, because they all knew those were his stomping grounds where he was heavily guarded by his sex, money, murder crew.

"That's all I know, I swear, papi. I don't know nothing," she cried. Her phone was ringing inside her bra. D Fatal Brim dug into her bra, pulling out her phone to see it was Glock on a FaceTime call, so he answered.

"Yooo, Glock, what's good, my guy? As you see, I got your baby mama," D Fatal Brim said, getting on FaceTime.

"Glock, help me, please!" Yasmine yelled before Paco kicked her in her face.

"Let her go, you bitch ass nigga, come see me like a man," Glock said on the phone

"I'll see you in traffic."

Boc, Boc, Boc, Boc, Boc, Boc...

D Fatal Brim shot Yasmine in her face, head, and upper torso while Glock was still on the phone.

"Nooo!" Glock yelled before he was disconnected.

"Bro, you wilding, you know how them iPhones are," Paco said.

"Fuck it," D Fatal Brim said, walking out the warehouse.

***

Soundview Projects, Bronx
1 Week Later

This was Glock's hood and the place where he grew up with his mom, brothers, and sister.

Glock's real name was Jeff Wald. He was a Blood gang member under a set called Sex, Money, Murder, which was heavy in Soundview thanks to the legend Pete.

At the age of thirty, all he knew was the streets and getting money to survive. He had a big crew of hitters all over the BX who loved him because of all the good he did for his homies.

He was medium height, high yellow, bald, and slim, with a goatee and a lazy eye, so he always wore sunglasses, even in the winter.

Working under Fats for a decade, he was able to get rich and put his crew on Bankroll, Big Blazer, who was upstate on a gun charge, and Pop-Off, who was the hottest rapper coming out of New York.

There was a big basketball game in the back of his projects. Over two hundred niggas were out, even two NBA stars from the hood. The buildings were all skyrises with twenty floors in each building. Glock didn't even want to come today, but he hadn't been out of his crib since the death of his baby mother.

He sent his son to go live with his sister up north in Albany for his safety, because he was about to turn the city up. Glock and D Fatal Brim had been beefing over a bitch named Chanel.

Glock knew it was D Fatal Brim and his crew robbing his people, his uncle and Fats, which was a big surprise because Fats ran a tight ship.

There weren't too many niggas out in the city robbing except D Fatal Brim and his crew, whom every drug dealer feared even hearing his name.

Tonight, Glock was going to bring D Fatal Brim a move in his own hood, Michelle, but he knew D Fatal Brim had been hanging out in Jackson projects, which was across the street from Michelle projects.

***

Jackson PJ, Bx
Later that night

"I'm taking all bets, Blood, all bets, you heard!" Too Live Balla shouted while shooting dice on the wall in the back parking lot where everybody hung out at.

"Put up 10 bandz, broke ass nigga!" D Fatal Brim shouted with a dark-skin, sexy bitch under his arm he brought out from Brooklyn.

"Damn, Brim, why you always do that?" Hev Balla said, who was D Fatal Brim's childhood friend.

"I got 10, bro, big bank take little bank. What's poppin', we got a bet, Hat Boy?" D Fatal Brim asked Too Live Balla in front of a crowd of niggas.

"Aight," Too Live Balla said in a raspy voice, handing D Fatal Brim the dice knowing he was about to crack him and take all

$7,500 on the ground. D Fatal Brim was nice wit' the dice and everybody knew that.

D Fatal Brim was up, and his crew, but he wanted more. He had jack boy dreams. The keys he and Knight got from Glock's uncle, they gave to Less, Black, and Paco to split.

Before the dice could even hit the wall after leaving D Fatal Brim's hand, shots rang out from every direction like an ambush.

Bloc, Bloc, Bloc, Bloc, Bloc, Bloc, Bloc!

Tat-tat-tat-tat-tat-tat-tat!

D Fatal Brim grabbed Too Live Balla and used him as a shield while shooting at the gunmen. He hit two, but there were still sixteen or more left, all with red flags on their faces.

Bloc, Bloc, Bloc, Bloc... Bloc, Bloc, Bloc, Bloc...

Hev Balla hit three gunmen back to back until he caught four shots to his head.

D Fatal Brim fired the rest of his bullets at the shooters as they filled Too Live Balla's lifeless body up with rounds.

"Shit." D Fatal Brim threw the empty gun and ran in the building, dodging bullets. Once inside, he called Knight, hearing tires screeching out the back lot leaving over a dozen bodies.

Romell Tukes

Chapter 5

Bayview Hotel, Bronx

"Ohhhh, shit, gimme that dick," Grace said, bouncing her nice, perfect brown ass up and down on D Fatal Brim's dick.

Her pussy was wet and warm, she wasn't tight but she wasn't loose. He held on to her waist as he guided her hips up and down, giving her every inch, hitting her G-spot.

"Fuck me, baby!" she screamed, kissing him.

They met two weeks ago in a lounge in Manhattan. Since then, they went on two dates and talked on the phone daily.

Grace was from the Bronx. She was in her mid-forties but she looked twenty. She was fit, petite with an ample ass, nice perky breasts, hazel eyes, long, jet-black hair mixed with tracks, a nice smile, and sex appeal.

D Fatal Brim finished beating her pussy up and he let her take a smoke break.

"I gotta see you again, Randall." She called him by his real name. She was grown and liked grown men.

"Anytime, love, just hit my line," he replied, getting dressed so he could go meet up with his little brother, Less, on Webster.

"Ok, handsome," she said, putting on her Prada slip-on dress and six-inch heels, looking beautiful.

Grace was on D Fatal Brim's body for a couple of months now, but he never had the right time to bag her. She was Glock's mother, and D Fatal Brim had to have her.

He nutted in her over three times tonight, hoping to put a seed in her just to make Glock mad. Grace knew her son was a kingpin, but she didn't know who he had beef with.

***

City Island, Co-op City

City Island was a strip full of seafood restaurants and it was always packed.

Kizzy was on a double date with his girlfriend, Yvette, who was a good girl in the nursing field. Yvette was twenty years old and sexy. She was Indian, Haitian, and African-American. Her smooth honey skin, long silky hair, chinky eyes, curves, and phat ass drove niggas crazy, but her heart was only for Kazzy. They met two years ago at a house party in Burnside and since then, they'd been an item.

Kip Loc's girl, Karen, was ratchet, straight from Michelle projects. She and Kip had been together since the fourth grade.

Karen was twenty-one years old, bisexual, light skin, and petite, with big breasts, thick eyebrows, and three tongue rings.

"This is good, baby," Karen said, eating fried whiting fish and oysters.

"Factz, we gotta come out here more," Kip Loc stated.

"Nigga, you know we ain't coming back out here," Kazzy said.

"Boy, shut up, you always ruining a good time," Yvette stated, drinking her soda.

"I gotta go to work, baby," Karen said, who was a bottle girl at a club in Queens.

"Okay, we out, cuz," Kip Loc said, seeing two niggas wearing big Cuban-link chains and Rolexes.

Kazzy Loc saw the look on Kip Loc's face and knew what he was on.

"I gotta go to the little girls' room," Yvette said, getting up.

"I'm about on them niggas, cuz," Kip Loc said, walking out the restaurant.

"You tripping, cuz," Kazzy Loc stated, following his homie outside, knowing what time it was.

Kip Loc caught up with the two niggas in the parking lot who were dripping with jewelry.

"Yoo, cuz," Kip Loc stated, six feet behind the two Bloods dripping in red Gucci outfits.

Both men turned around to see two guns pointed at their face.

Kip Loc and Kazzy Loc snatched off both of their chains.

28

"Take off your watches, cuz," Kazzy Loc stated.

"Damn, Blood," one of them stated, taking off his watch.

Yvette and Karen came walking past them and stopped.

"Oh hell no, Kazzy!" Yvette yelled, taking them out their zone.

When they got the watches, they walked off with the two girls while the two Blood niggas from Queens hopped in their BMW X5, pulling off.

***

Manhattan, NY

Tool was a local drug dealer from Lambert Projects, selling work for Glock. He was also a sex, money, murder member.

Today was Tool's birthday and he was in the jewelry store in the city. He was picking up his $85,000 Audemars Piguet Royal Oak-Chronograph limited edition.

Tool walked out the store smiling hard with his watch on his left wrist. He couldn't wait to hit the club later and stunt.

He parked his Camaro around the corner near an alley. He was so focused on his watch, he didn't see D Fatal Brim step out with his Glock out.

"What's poppin', you soft ass nigga," D Fatal Brim said with his gun to Tool, seeing the fear of God in him.

Tool had heard of D Fatal Brim, the whole Bronx had. He was the coldest robber in the city.

"Here, bro, just take it," Tool said, taking off his watch.

"I was going take it anyway, son."

Boc, Boc!

After killing Tool, D Fatal Brim took the watch and placed it on his wrist, walking off. D Fatal was on his way to buy some jewelry until he saw Tool coming out the store, now he had a free watch.

Romell Tukes

Chapter 6

Mott Haven Projects, BX

Black pulled up to the side block leading into the Mott Haven projects. He turned off his Nissan while Less smoked on a blunt of loud they just got from Washington Heights.

They also copped two gallons of Nutcrackers, which was a tasty, strong liquor.

Black met a bitch on Fordham two days ago and she told him she was trying to get up, and she had a sister. Black brought Less along so they could go out somewhere and chill.

When she told Black she lived in Mott Haven, he told her he wasn't going inside the pjs, but he'd meet her and her sister on the side block next to the projects.

Black and Less were both Mack Ballas, and Mott Haven niggas hated them, so going in there was a death trap.

"Yo, son, where these hoes at?" Less said, looking down the dark block, not liking this idea, but he was coming for his boy because he knew how Mott Haven bitches gave it up.

"Chill, boy, they coming skrap," Black said, texting the chick he met. He didn't even know her name.

Less looked out his door mirror to see three niggas creeping down the block.

"Bro, it's a trap, it's lite." Less grabbed his Glock 18 with the fully extended clip, and Black pulled out his P89 Ruger.

They climbed out the car at the same time with a drop and roll movement, firing towards the gunmen, hitting one in his face.

Bloc, Bloc, Bloc, Bloc, Bloc, Bloc...

Boc, Boc, Boc, Boc... BOOM, BOOM...

Less's leg got grazed, but he continued to fire round after round until he killed the tall gunman.

The last gunman wasn't letting up. He was going bullet for bullet with Black until sirens could be heard from a distance.

When they saw the shooter run off, they climbed back in the Nissan with the push-to-start button.

"You see where being thirsty for some pussy get you, goofy ass nigga," Less said, laughing but serious, as he wrapped a red flag over the small cut he got from being grazed.

***

Minutes Later

"Yo, son, they just hit Burn and Puff Da Gunner," PG said, rushing in the crib in the back building of Mott Haven projects.

"Fuck, how you let that happen?" YG said, counting stacks of money from a long day of work.

LaLa and Keisha both sat on the couch listening, glad they didn't go outside to meet them.

LaLa met Black on Fordham, she was YG and PG's sister. When she asked them about Black from Mill Brook, they had her set him up. Lala was young, cute, light skin, and thick, with short hair, and was a thot.

"Them niggas saw us coming. What the fuck you mean, bro? I see your scary ass ain't go out there," PG said, walking to the back.

"If I would have went out them niggas would be dead, and that's on the G'z!" YG shouted, texting Glock to tell him it's all bad.

PG and YG were brothers, but nobody would ever know because they were like night and day.

PG was twenty years old, tall, fat, and ugly, with light-brown skin. He ran with a crew who called themselves Gunnerz, and so did YG, his older brother. YG was twenty-one years old, tall, brown skin, handsome, tatted up, skinny, and a hothead.

YG's real name was YaYa, and PG's real name was Abullah. Both men had the same father and mother. Their father was killed in the army just days after their sister was born.

They sold drugs for Glock, and they were his young boys about that gun play. Glock had $100,000 on D Fatal Brim and Knight's crew. YG knew who was down with them, the whole city did, because they were vicious niggas.

***

Brooklyn, NY

Pop-Off was in the studio booth recording for his third album EP. Pop-Off was one of the best rappers to come out of the Bronx in the past year. He had Hot 97 radio station going crazy. He was waiting on a deal with Def Jam to go through, or Ruff Ryders.

He was from Soundview and his little sister was Yvette, who was Kazzy Loc's wifey, but he didn't know who his sister was dating.

Pop-Off was twenty-seven, brown skinned, and medium height, with waves and a chipped tooth. He had a Nas look and flow on the mic. He was Sex, Money, Murder under Big Blazer.

Glock was the one who helped put Pop-Off in the rap game. He took care of all his fines for his studio time, albums, and marketing. Pop-Off was still in the streets, one foot in and one foot out.

"That's it for today, homie!" his engineer shouted before leaving the room after saving everything.

Pop-Off stepped foot out the booth to see Bankroll, who was his cousin and Glock's best friend, standing there.

"Good one, I enjoyed that, son. We gotta go holler at Flex and get him to do the bomb like twenty times on that, son," Bankroll said, being honest.

Bankroll was well respected around the New York City area. He had a long trail of bodies and he beat four on two different trials. At twenty-five, he was focused on a bag, and he had his hood, Soundview, on lock.

Bankroll was short, bald, with a high-yellow complexion, and very quiet.

"I'm about to go check Glock about D Fatal Brim and Knight. This shit about to get brazy, blazer, and I want you to stay out of this. I know how loyal you are to us, but you about to make it and put on for us, bro," Bankroll stated, knowing how much Pop-Off loved the bros.

"Aight, bro, tell Glock I send my blazer love," Pop-Off said.

"Say less. I'm out," Bankroll said, leaving with three chains swagging on his neck, wishing a nigga would try him.

Pop-Off sat down thinking about what happened to Tool, who was his right-hand man, but he didn't want to end up like him.

When he heard Glock was beefing with D Fatal Brim and Knight, he knew it was going to be a crazy bloodbath. Pop-Off also knew Kazzy Loc, Kip Loc, Paco, Less, and Black were all official hitters.

He was confused about whether he should focus on this rap shit, everything he worked so hard for, or ride with the streets, his gang and bros.

Pop-Off grabbed his Louis Vuitton backpack with his 9mm handgun inside and left.

Chapter 7

White Plains, NY

D Fatal Brim and his brother, Less, sat in the Cheesecake Factory eating and drinking while D Fatal Brim schooled his little brother.

"Tell me who your best friends are and I'll tell you who you are, Blood. If you run with wolves, you will learn how to bowl. But if you associate with eagles, you will learn how to soar to great heights. A mirror reflects a man's face, but what he is really like is shown by the kind of friends he chooses," D Fatal Brim stated.

"True, fact of life, bro, but I know who to associate with. I fuck with my day ones," Less replied.

"The less you associate with some people, the more your life will improve. I hate you chose the streets, bro, you and Kip, but I want to see you both succeed in life," D Fatal Brim said, eating steak.

"I know."

"Friends that don't help you climb will want you to crawl. Niggas will stretch your vision or choke your dream," D Fatal Brim stated, being honest, seeing it happen many times.

"That's why I move how a G supposed to," Less said, seeing Black blow his phone up. They chilled for another half an hour and left, heading back to the Bronx thinking about their next dollar.

***

Melrose Projects, BX

Paco was getting dressed while looking at the two bad Spanish bitches sleep in his bed. Paco lived in the hood with Hasley and Katty, who were both bisexual and dancers in the hottest strip club in New York City.

Both women were Dominican, twenty-two, and in love with Paco. They'd been with him in a three-way relationship for two years now and loved every second of it.

The women knew Paco's lifestyle and they were down for him. They killed, robbed, and set niggas up for him.

Paco loved both women the same, they meant a lot to him. He got both their names tatted, and they both got his name tatted also. They were both overprotective of him and were jealous any time any other women came in the picture, but they played it cool because they knew Paco's heart was only for them. Hasley and Katty both had their bodies done.

Hasley was taller and bronze, with blonde hair, a phat ass, tattoos, green eyes, nice perky breasts, and full lips.

Katty was short and had chinky hazel eyes, big titties, a big, fake ass, long jet-black hair, deep dimples, and a nice bright smile with a tongue and lip ring.

"Papi, you leaving?" Katty asked, getting up.

"Yeah, I'm using your Benz. Call me later," Paco said, putting his pistol in his lower back.

"Ok, I love you," Katty said, laying back down.

"Love the both of you. Go back to sleep," Paco said, placing his hair in a ponytail, leaving to go meet Less and Black.

***

Washington Ave, BX
Hours Later

"My brother said that's her in the black dress talking to that stocky nigga in the front," Less said, looking at a picture of Grace on his iPhone.

"Damn, she fire, bro," Black said, watching Grace in the front of the lounge on the corner drinking, having a good time.

"Nigga, you shutting, bro," Paco said from the driver's seat of Katty's Benz she worked the pole to get.

"Everybody can't fuck two bad bitches like you, brotty, and I'm trying to fuck either one of them," Black replied, watching Glock's mom.

"Them bitches wouldn't fuck you with my dick, and you look like the type of nigga to burn a bitch," Paco said, making Less laugh.

"That was one time!" Black yelled, getting defensive.

"What's up with that plug nigga in the Heights, Paco?" Less asked, knowing he needed a new lick soon. His brother gave him a key but he sold it to a man from Burnside for the low and copped a new BMW.

"Word, son, because I just spent the rest of my bread on a bust down, big face AP," Black said, seeing Grace cross the street about to head to her car.

"Soon, but the bros, Kazzy Loc and Kip Loc, is in his nephew line, so I'ma figure it out, but there she go," Paco said, seeing Grace twenty feet away.

Black and Less jumped out with the ski masks on.

Boc, Boc, Boc, Boc, Bloc, Bloc, Bloc...

Grace didn't even see what hit her as they killed her in front of her Lexus.

Black and Less jumped back in the Benz, racing off in the opposite direction of the lounge so nobody would see them. D Fatal Brim sent the hit. He could have done it himself, but he was schooling Less and his crew.

***

Hunts Point, BX

Lil' Killer, aka Lil' K, was with his crew on dirt bikes riding through Fox Lane on their way to the park, hoping they wouldn't run into police, or it was going to be a chase.

Lil' K was seventeen, tall, handsome, and lean, with brown skin and long dreads he'd been growing for ten years. The ladies loved him. He was Knight and Kazzy Loc's little brother. He had his own little crew and all they did was ride dirt bikes and sell weed dimes and ounces.

When they got to the park, which was a safe haven for bikes, all four bikes stopped.

"What we doing tonight?" Red said, stepping off her dirt bike.

Red was Lil' K's best friend. She was mixed, black and white, so she was high yellow with green eyes that had brown in them, medium height, and long hair that dropped to her ass. She was a bad bitch but everybody thought she was gay, but she disliked males and females. She and her brother, Banger, were both from Uptown around Gun Hill Road.

Banger was sixteen, in high school, and one of the best point guards in the Bronx. He was very tall and skinny, and had waves and nice charm. His best friend was Bugatti, who was also sixteen.

Bugatti was from Eastchester Gardens. He was Blood, an Ape under his big brother, Eighty, who was in prison for life for a body. Bugatti was short, dark, husky, short tempered, and had long braids.

All of them except Banger dropped out of school. There was another member, Blu, who was on Rikers Island for a gun charge. He was 16 years old.

"Let's go fuck wit' them Edenwald niggas," Banger stated, sitting on his bike.

"Them niggas jumped Duke two nights ago, like seven Blood Hand niggas. Hell nah, I ain't going over there," Bugatti stated.

"I am, ask Kazzy for the grip," Lil' K said.

"That nigga ain't giving you no gun, and you know Knight not," Red said, knowing his brothers well because she spent nights over his house for years.

"Let's go to RPT," Lil' K said, jumping on his bike, riding off.

Chapter 8

3rd Ave, Bronx

Pop-Off was walking down 3rd Ave shopping district with his man Grippy from his hood.

"Yoo, bro, SoundCloud going crazy over that 'We Bangin' song," Grippy stated, walking into Sneaker World to see all the hottest new shoes on stands and hanging from the walls.

"That shit going to have the city lit, bro. I'm just focused on this Def Jam meeting in a couple of weeks, son," Pop-Off said, looking at a thick Spanish bitch eye his chain, which was a Jesus piece.

"How much you think they talking?"

"Niggas be thinking rappers be signing for millions and shit, but that's not true, son. Niggas be getting them advancements that they eventually will have to pay back," Pop-Off said, picking up a new pair of Air Max 95, red and black.

"Nigga, fuck all that, how much you shooting for, Blood? Because you out here spitting harder than any of these goofy niggas," Grippy said seriously.

"I'll do 500,000," Pop-Off said, shrugging his shoulders.

"What? Nigga, you bugging the fuck out. My nigga Glock making that shit in two days in the hood. Why lower your value, bro?" Grippy said as Pop-Off grabbed a red Yankees New Era hat and went to the cash register.

"Bro, I ain't Glock, Bankroll, Big Blazer, or Wooh, son. I'm me, and I'ma get in the industry the right way," Pop-Off stated as Grippy nodded his head.

Grippy was still in the streets running crazy, but he hung around Pop-Off because he knew sooner or later Pop-Off was going to be something big.

Walking out the store, Grippy and Pop-Off ran straight into Black and some tall, slim, dark-skin bitch walking with him.

Grippy pulled out his gun while Black did the same. Black pushed the chick in front of the men as shots started to fly.

Bloc, Bloc, Bloc, Bloc, Bloc, Bloc, Bloc...

Boc, Boc, Boc, Boc, Boc, Boc, Boc...

Black hid inside of a store, firing shots, hitting Grippy three times and the chick. Pop-Off saw Grippy go down and he fired towards Black but missed, trying not to hit a civilian.

Black shot two shots at Pop-Off, seeing civilians run screaming during the mayhem.

Two NYPD cops were running up the street, making both men scatter within the crowds, leaving Grippy's dead body and Black's friend he met minutes ago.

***

181st and Ryer Ave, BX

Kazzy had Yvette's legs all over his shoulders as he pounded her pretty little pussy out, making her go crazy.

"Oh shit, zaddy," she moaned, grabbing her sheets from behind her head.

Kazzy loved when her pussy muscles clenched onto his manhood every time he went in her, but it made it hard to control himself.

Yvette loved missionary because she liked to look into his eyes while getting fucked.

When it was time to change positions, she climbed on his dick in the reverse cowgirl.

"Ahhh... Uhmmmm, fuck," she cried, feeling every inch sink into her waterfall.

Yvette started to slow grind on his dick, bouncing up and down as if she was dancing.

"Kaz-z-zzyyy!" she screamed, feeling herself about to climax as he gripped her ass, sliding his dick in and out at a rapid speed, making her breasts bounce up and down.

Yvette came hard, out of breath and sore from him pounding out her pussy. She saw Kazzy's dick was still hard and she couldn't take any more.

"I'm sorry, baby, but you going to have to jerk off," Yvette said, getting dressed, reading a text from her girlfriend Cynthia saying there was a big shooting on 3rd Ave and Grippy was killed.

"I'll call Tamika," he said with a smirk.

"What? Nigga, stop playing with me," Yvette stated seriously, being gangsta.

"I'm just playing, but I gotta go to the hood and holler at my mom. She been asking about you," Kazzy stated, putting on his Fendi hoodie.

"You heard about Grippy?"

"Nah."

"Niggas just killed him on 3rd Ave in broad daylight. This shit getting wicked out here," she said, getting ready for work.

"Shit crazy out here, babe." Kazzy knew who Grippy was, but he would never tell her. Kazzy never met Yvette's family and she never talked about them. He felt as if there was another life to her. She was very private but Kazzy respected her privacy as a woman.

Yvette had a good job, a bag, her own crib, and a nice new Lexus coupe. She was his dream girl and she was his rider. He loved everything about her.

"You staying over here tonight when you get back from doing whatever you doing?" she asked.

"I'ma stay at my mom's crib. I ain't been home in two days. You know how mama love is."

"Mama's boy," she mumbled.

"What?" Kazzy said, getting serious.

"Nothing, babe," she said with a chuckle. Kazzy was a true mama's boy and everybody knew that.

***

Soundview, Bronx

Kazzy Loc was sitting in Paco's new Charger watching their target creep into the apartment complex. It was 11:30 p.m. on a Sunday night and it was the perfect time to catch a nigga slipping.

"How you get the do on Wooh?" Paco asked.

"I know one of his feins. He from my building but moved to Soundview. Let's wait until he come out?" Kazzy asked.

"Hell nah, bro, we about to pull up on there," Paco said, putting on his mask. Kazzy said fuck it and followed Paco.

***

Wooh was a big, black, gorilla-looking nigga with no neck. He was in the kitchen placing keys under his kitchen sink. Wooh worked for Glock, his cousin.

"Big boy, what's popping?" Kazzy said with his Glock pointed at him. Wooh was scared. Words couldn't even come out of his lips. Paco saw all the keys on the table and knew they hit the jackpot.

"Get down on the floor, bitch nigga," Paco said while Kazzy moved in to bag up all the keys and stacks of money wrapped in plastic under the counter. Kazzy saw Wooh's face fighting him while he put everything in the two duffle bags.

Boc, Boc, Boc, Boc...

Wooh's head popped off like a can top.

"Damn, son," Paco said, seeing blood on his tan Timberlands.

"My bad," Kazzy said, laughing. They left the crib, excited.

***

Two Blocks Away
Soundview, BX

"You think the money in his Audi?" Black asked Knight as they watched Lil' Rod's tail lights go off on a side block, as if he was waiting on someone.

"Nigga, please stop talking, just follow my lead, son," Knight said, jumping out the Infiniti Q60.

***

Lil' Rod was waiting on Bankroll to pull up wit' the work. He was coping 17 bricks with $200,000, and Glock was gonna let him slide for the rest.

Lil' Rod was Big Blazer's nephew, and he was getting money on Soundview. He was counting money out his Louis Vuitton backpack. When he heard the knock on his window, he almost had a heart attack. There was a knock on his other window, and he rolled down his window with no choice.

"Keep your hands up," Knight stated as Black snatched the passenger door open and snatched the Louis Vuitton bag off his seat.

"Yo, son, don't take my life—"

Boc, Boc, Boc, Boc, Boc...

Lil' Rod's neck blew off into the passenger seat. Black saw smoke coming from Knight's gun. He was shocked to see him smoke son, because that wasn't the plan. They left the crime scene in no rush, seeing a real G-wagon pass them, which was Bankroll.

Romell Tukes

Chapter 9

Forest Projects, Bronx

JayJay was Glock's younger brother, who was twenty-seven years old living a square life. JayJay was a family man with a beautiful wife and two sons.

Unlike his brother, whom he had no ties with, JayJay gave his life to Islam years ago and was a faithful Muslim.

JayJay had his CDL license and drove 18 wheelers and commercial trucks for a big company in Hunts Point.

It was 6 am and JayJay was on his way to work, walking into his building parking lot. This was his everyday routine. He would stop at McDonald's for coffee and make his way to work.

His hours were 7 am-11 pm seven days a week, but at 27 dollars an hour, he never complained.

A man dressed in a Nike Tech hoodie was walking towards him. "You JayJay?" the man asked.

"Yeah, who wants to know?" JayJay said, getting on defensive mode.

When he saw the man in the hoodie pull out a gun, he almost shitted himself.

"Wooow! Look, man, I'm not with that life. I'm a God-fearing man," JayJay said, raising his hand, swallowing a spit ball as he looked into the man's cold eyes.

"This ain't got nothing to do wit' you, son, you heard."
Bloc! Bloc! Bloc! Bloc!
JayJay slammed into the hood of his new red Acura sedan.
D Fatal Brim jogged out the projects down Union Ave.

***

Millbrook Pjs, Bx
Two Days Later

Black and Kazzy were posted up on 137th and Brook Ave, in front of the Ock store they shot dice and sold drugs in front of.

The Ocks who ran the store were from Syria and they were official. They let niggas hide guns and drugs in the store when the police watch came through.

Niggas even ran trains on bitches in the back of the store as long as the Ocks could get some pussy also.

It was 8:30 pm and everybody was trying to figure out their plans for the night while shooting dice on the wall smoking bud. The whole crew was dressed in designer clothes with Timbs or Airmax 95s on their feet.

The money Black got off the robbery he did with Knight was a big lick, and the keys. They divided up everything from their lick and Paco and Kazzy's lick, so everybody was now sitting on a nice amount of money and drugs.

"Let's go out to Brooklyn, boy. I ain't tryna stay in da X tonight," Black said, blowing smoke clouds of loud into the air.

"I gotta go out there to holler at the crips anyway," Kazzy Loc stated as Black just looked at him.

"Bro, you know niggas don't fuck with wild crip niggas out there, we all Bloods. If a nigga ain't the Prime, Jet, Hound, or Mad Hatter or da Ape, then niggas ain't tryna chill in niggas' hoods. Especially no hardbacks," Black said.

"Look, cuz, disrespect my shit one more time and we can get it in right here," Kazzy Loc stated, feeling like Black was trying to disrespect his crip set.

"What the fuck you mean, nigga, it's whatever," Black said, now face to face with his childhood friend as niggas watched, placing money on Kazzy Loc because his hand game was serious.

Black always disliked crips because a crip killed his older brother years ago in Long Island.

Before either man could swing, shots rang out from across the street. Four hitters in all black sprayed rounds from Dracos.

Black pulled out his Glock 17 with the 30 rounds, hiding behind an old pick-up truck, hitting one of the gunmen, taking him out.

Kazzy Loc duck walked with his Tech 9, hitting two gunmen.
Tat-tat-tat-tat-tat-tat-tat...

The last shooter was hitting niggas off left and right. Bankroll already killed four niggas in front of the store.

Bankroll saw Black pop out from behind the pick-up truck, hitting him in his arm.

"Ahhhh Ahhhh, bitch!" Black yelled, hitting the ground. Kazzy Loc and two of his guys tried to take Bankroll's head clean off, but he was ducking, dodging, zig-zagging, and running down the block trying to get low.

Sirens could be heard, so everybody ran off. Kazzy helped Black off the floor, taking him to building 165 to the sixth floor where his old babysitter, Aunty Jamie, was a licensed nurse. Everybody went to her for medical attention.

***

Morehouse Pjs, Bronx
Next Night

Morehouse projects were under Glock's control. He was moving over twenty keys every three days in the projects with Gyro's help.

Gyro was an older Nine-Tray Blood gang member who was always in prison for dumb shit. He was Glock's man, so Glock looked out for him. Gyro had his hood on lock, twelve workers, four stash cribs in the back building, and a crew of shooters.

It was broad daylight outside and today was a slow business day.

"Yo, what's poppin' wit' Arrow the Billy, why y'all niggas ain't put that money on the books like I asked?" Gyro stated, walking out the front building with two flanks.

"My bad, Gyro, I forgot," Law P said.

"Me too, bro, I'ma send it."

Whop... Whop...

Gyro slapped both men in their faces, which echoed through the whole projects.

"Get the fuck off the block. If I ever see y'all niggas down here, I'ma stick my dick in y'all mouths," Gyro stated as his two goons he came out the building with looked at each other, because that wasn't the first time he said some crazy gay shit.

"Pause, no homo," Gyro said, turning to go back in the building because he forgot his phone. "I'll be right back, son. Zip and Gram are supposed to pull up, just make them wait. I left my phone in the trap," Gyro said, walking into the building.

He always took the staircase because the project elevator always got stuck, and he was only going to the second floor. When he got to the second floor, two armed men rushed him.

PSST, PSST, PSST, PSST, PSST, PSST, PSST!

Gyro niftily fell back into the staircase, and Paco and Knight walked down the staircase and put two bullets in his head because he was still breathing.

Paco and Knight snuck through the back exit, after a fein gave up Gyro's location for an 8 ball. They were gonna kick in his door, but when they saw him coming through the staircase, it was on and poppin'. Knight and D Fatal Brim were on Glock's line. They were going after all of his main workers and killers. Fats was nowhere to be found, so he wasn't their focus anymore.

Chapter 10

Washington Heights, NY

Paco walked into the small Spanish restaurant to see two older men playing chess while two big Spanish guards stood on the wall watching Paco's every move.

Paco was going to speak Spanish, but he thought against it.

"Excuse me, is Carlos here?" Paco asked while the shorter Dominican man with the gray hair placed one finger in the air, giving him a hint to wait.

Katty told Paco about her uncle Carlos and about how much weight he was moving in the Heights, which was her worst mistake.

Paco sweet talked her into having her set up a sit down with Carlos and him.

Carlos was a coke plug in the Heights. He was rich and had plenty of work to feed every drug dealer in New York.

"Good game, Carlos," Joseph stated, getting up from the table to leave while taking one good look at Paco.

"Your name's Paco, right?"

"Yeah, thank you for inviting me," Paco said, taking a seat while the old man stared into his eyes trying to read his soul, something he always did when meeting someone for the first time.

"Katty tells me you're getting a little money and need some help?" Carlos stated, smoothly pulling out a Cuban cigar and a lighter from his shirt pocket.

"Yeah, I'm trying to get up to 100 keys," Paco stated, making Carlos laugh.

"You got high dreams, I like that, kid. How many bricks you moving now?" Carlos said, catching him off guard, because he had nothing at the moment. He sold his drugs from his previous robbery to his homie in Queens he went to school with, who he was getting money with.

"I'm moving ten a week," Paco stated as Carlos looked at him with a smirk.

"So, you don't know a man named Knight or D Fatal Brim?" Carlos stated as his two guards came closer towards them with their guns drawn.

"I never heard of them," Paco said, keeping his cool, looking at his goons.

"It seems to me my connect thinks differently, Paco. When Katty told me about you over the phone, I had to look into you, because my niece is a snake just like her mother, and snakes sleep in the same pits. That same day, my plug, Fats, was here and he told me you are down with the crew who goes around robbing drug dealers. But look, you fell into my web," Carlos said, pulling out his phone to call Fats.

"I like your style, old man, but you gotta try a little harder to catch me lackin'," Paco said.

"What!" Carlos said, trying to figure out the meaning behind his words.

BOOM... BOOM...

Both of the guards' heads exploded like a balloon.

Carlos's eyes widened with fear as Knight and D Fatal Brim walked in from the back exit after tying up two workers in the back.

Two shotguns were trained on Carlos now as Paco stated in Spanish, asking him where the stash was.

"Y'all niggas need to talk in English," Knight stated, not knowing what was going on.

"He said everything is in the bathroom ceiling already in duffle bags," Paco said, pulling out his P89 Ruger, firing four rounds in Carlos's forehead while Knight and D Fatal Brim went to the bathroom.

***

An Hour Later

Everybody was in Less's crib counting money and kilos.

"Yo, we been hitting these, cuz," Kip Loc said, separating the money and drugs into seven piles.

"This is how this shit supposed to be done," D Fatal Brim stated, looking at all the stacks of money and coke.

"Facts, bro," Less stated.

"How much that is, Blood, for everybody?" Black stated.

"Seventeen keys apiece and $225,000 for everybody," Kip Loc said.

Kazzy wanted to jump up and down, and so did everybody else in the room.

***

Burnside, Bronx
One Week

D Fatal Brim copped a new Porsche truck and had been knocking off keys all over the city. He just dropped off five to his bro, Trust, he did a bid with years ago.

Everything in his life was going perfect. He felt like all his years of hard work finally paid off, and to see his little brothers eating made him feel stronger. Family was important to him, and his brothers and Knight were all he had.

Two detective cars blocked his Porsche in. D Fatal Brim panicked and slammed into the black Ford Taurus twice, getting out the box, racing off down the street pressing Harris Ave.

The two cop cars and two patrol cars were now on his tail as he whipped the Porsche through the busy street, University Ave, going 110 mph, almost hitting bystanders.

D Fatal Brim reached under his seat to get his pistol to shoot it out with the police, but he couldn't feel it. He was swerving in and out of traffic as a line of police cars was in high pursuit.

An 18-wheeler came out the alley, and the Porsche crashed right into it, smashing the Porsche's windows, hood, and front side. The windows were all gone as the car spun around. When the police made it to D Fatal Brim, he looked dead. The ambulance came right away, trying to save his life, but he had no pulse as they rushed him to the hospital.

Chapter 11

Manhattan, NY

Pop-Off walked out of Def Jam's building, after just signing a big three-album deal with no budget. Pop-Off's A&R and manager got him a sitdown with the label last week, and he waited until this day.

He sat at a round table with six other head officials in the label listening to his new album and two mixtapes.

They even asked him to perform in front of everybody. He killed the performance and had everybody going crazy.

When his Uber pulled up, he jumped in, texting everybody letting niggas know he was on and ready to turn the city up.

His manager told him in a couple of weeks, they would be going to Miami to record another album for the label.

***

Jacoby Hospital, Bronx

D Fatal Brim was chained to the hospital bed, surrounded by IVs and machines. He saw a gang of police officers outside his door.

He was lucky to be alive after his accident. He was banged up pretty bad. He had a serious concussion and was still in critical condition.

"Fatal Brim, the big homie," a cop stated, walking in the room in a suit.

"What the fuck you want, pig?" D Fatal Brim said in a low-pitched voice because his body was still fucked up.

"You are under arrest for the murder of Yasmine Jefferson. This is your federal indictment of one count of murder," the cop said, flashing his FBI badge.

"Feds?" D Fatal Brim stated, shocked the feds got him.

"Yeap, we got you now, and I'm looking into more cases. You robbed a lot of major people we have under our scope, and you and your crew also killed a lot of people we were watching."

"You ain't got shit on me, pig, suck my dick," D Fatal Brim said.

"That's where you're wrong. We have you on FaceTime killing Yasmine, saying I'll see you in traffic," the FBI agent stated.

D Fatal Brim was stuck because he remembered those words he told Glock before killing his baby mother.

"It came back to you, I see."

"Fuck you, bitch," D Fatal Brim said as the FBI agent walked out of the room.

D Fatal Brim knew how hard it was to beat the feds, so he knew he had a fight ahead of him.

"Oh, yeah, we got a gun charge for you too," the agent said, peeking his head back in the room with a smile.

***
183rd, Bronx

Black was on the four train platform waiting for the train to come so he could go to Mount Vernon to buy a car from his cousin who was a salesman at a car dealership.

He pulled out a cigarette but realized he didn't have a lighter. A nigga was walking down the stairs and Black walked towards him.

Black was getting money selling keys for the low in Webster projects. Today, he was going to cop a nice car to get around in.

This morning, he heard about D Fatal Brim's arrest when Less told him D Fatal Brim was all over the news. Black was scared, wondering if the feds were coming for him and everybody else.

"You got a lighter, fam?" Black said, looking at the man's face, which looked familiar but he couldn't pinpoint it.

When the man saw Black's face, he reached for his gun instead of a lighter. Black saw his movement and punched him in the face, making him back pedal. Black pulled out his gun and fired two shots, hitting the stairwell.

PG got his balance then hid behind the stairs, firing four shots but hitting the pole in the middle of the platform where Black hid.

PG was on his way to Harlem to meet up with a chick he'd been dealing with for years, when he ran into Black.

Boc! Boc! Boc! Boc! Boc!

"Shit," Black said, dodging PG's bullets. Black fired two shots and ran down towards the end of the platform and ran down the stairs as bullets missed him. With only two bullets left, Black took off, knowing he would eventually see PG again.

***

Mill Brook Projects, BX

Kazzy Loc and Less were posted in front of building 165 watching feins cop and go like a real candy store. The past two weeks, they'd been trapping hard trying to get rid of the bricks so they could get D Fatal Brim out of jail, because his bail was close to a million dollars.

The crew had been blowing money fast since robbing Carlos. The bricks were easy to bust down and sell in the hood because they had over thirteen workers in the projects.

"You spoke to Kip earlier?" Less asked, knowing if any nigga knew where his brother was it was his best friend.

"He in Brooklyn with the Locs. He said he just needed to get away. Everybody fucked up about D Fatal Brim, bro," Kazzy said, seeing two niggas with hoodies on rush inside of a GMC truck with two garbage bags. So many niggas walked through the projects he couldn't keep count, so he paid them no mind.

"Factz, I hope we can get home soon. Let's go upstairs so I can see how much we got all together. I don't trust that fein bitch crib, bro, we should move everything to Webster," Less said, walking into the building.

"Nigga, hell nah, that whole hood hot, bro. The feds just got sixteen Mackballers last week," Kazzy stated, walking down the hall to see apartment 3J1's door wide open.

Both men ran inside the crib to see crackhead Betty on the kitchen floor stabbed to death, laying in a puddle of blood.

"Check the stash!" Kazzy yelled, thinking about the two niggas he saw leaving the building minutes ago.

Less searched the back room closet up and down to see all the money and drugs were gone.

"It's gone, son," Less said, wanting to cry. Everybody's keys were stashed in that closet, and Less and Kazzy's money. Everybody else was blowing with nothing to show for it. Less and Kazzy left the building, calling Knight.

"That's what's up, bro, but this visit is over. Come see me whenever and be smart out there," D Fatal Brim said, seeing the CO ending prisoners' visits.

"Aight, I love you," Kip Loc said as he stood to leave.

D Fatal Brim went to the back to strip out like all the rest of the prisoners while the voice went off on the seventh floor.

The guards ran out the room to the fight going off upstairs. D Fatal Brim knew it had to be G they was fucking up. D Fatal Brim sat on the ground thinking about the free world.

***

Soundview Pjs, Bronx

Glock and Bankroll were in the projects playground sharing a bottle of liquor as they did since little niggas running around the hood, broke and dirty.

"Hitting them niggas' pockets was the biggest thing we could do, and now that bitch ass nigga, Fatal, locked up. Them niggas weak," Glock said, sitting on the bench looking at all the buildings that surrounded him.

"Don't sleep on Knight, he just as dangerous, if not more," Bankroll said seriously.

"Man, that nigga soft. Just 'cause he got a couple of bodies under his belt don't mean shit," Glock said, taking a sip out the bottle.

Bankroll knew he was just saying anything, running his mouth, but he let him chant until his jaw hurt.

Romell Tukes

Chapter 13

Burnside, Bronx

The nursing home on Harris Ave was the home of Mr. Wald, Glock's father, who was in his late seventies.

Mr. Wald had been there close to two years. Now, this was his home until his day came, and he was well ready for it. He was a deep-spirited Christian man raised in the heart of Alabama in a small town called Salem, where he marched with Martin Luther King Jr. in the early sixties, and John Lewis.

Today was a nice day and Mr. Wald was outside in the back watching the men cut the grass. Mr. Wald was in a wheelchair drinking a glass of water, thinking about the days when he was in the army fighting during World War II.

The two lawn workers approached Mr. Wald with their guns. *Boc, Boc, Boc, Boc, Boc, Boc!!!!!!*

One of the men shot Mr. Wald in the chest, killing him, before they ran off, jumping over the fence.

Knight and Kip Loc were acting like they were cutting the grass. Kip Loc knew killing Glock's father would hit him harder than anything.

***

Melrose Pjs, Bx

Paco was laying on his back while Hasley and Katty both shared his dick.

"Uhmmmmmm..." Hasley moaned, making love to his dick with her full lips as she bobbed her head up and down.

Hasley's pussy was being eaten by Katty, her tongue played with the ring pierced in Hasley's clit.

"Ohhh, fuck!" Hasley screamed while Katty hit her spot. Hasley swallowed Paco's whole dick, letting him feel her clench as she released her tonsils, deep throating him.

"Switch," Paco said, feeling himself about to nut in her wet mouth.

Katty stopped eating Hasley's pussy and took her position on his dick in a reverse cowgirl style while Hasley sucked on her pussy. Katty's pussy was wet and tight. She made her ass cheeks clap on his dick one side at a time like she did in the strip club.

"Ugghhh," Katty moaned as Paco palmed her ass, giving her all his dick inch by inch until he hit rock bottom.

Katty felt the pressure applied to her asshole as Hasley stuck her finger in her tiny back door, stretching her out.

"I'm coming, papi!" Katty screamed as she covered his dick with her coochie juices. Katty hopped off and Paco stood up.

Paco bent Hasley over roughly and rammed his dick deep into her phat pussy.

"Ahhhhhhh!" Hasley screamed, gripping the bed sheets. Katty grabbed Hasley by her hair and forced her face into her coochie so she could eat her out.

Hasley loved to be choked, manhandled, and roughed up. She took the dick like a champ while Paco pounded her back out for ten minutes, until she came and he shot his load in her.

"Damn, Paco, you was on one tonight, daddy," Hasley stated, seeing her edges were sweated out.

"No lie, my little pussy is still throbbing," Katty said, getting under the covers with Paco and Hasley. Paco didn't tell them he took a gram of Molly two hours ago, because they disliked when he did drugs.

"It's just one of them nights. I'm very happy to have two beautiful women I can love and fall asleep with every night," he said, laying in the middle of both of them.

"We love you too, papi," Katty stated.

"Always," Hasley added, lying on his chest.

For the past couple of weeks, Paco had been focused on blowing money and trying to plot his next move. When the stash house was robbed, he took a big hit because all of his keys were in there also, but luckily, he had a little money left to maintain.

Black told him in a couple of days he would have a power move set up for them and he couldn't wait, because he was getting bored robbing, and killing was a hobby to him.

***

Mott Haven Projects, BX

Bravo was YG and PG's uncle. He was a mid-level hustler, and at the age of thirty-two, he still acted like he was twenty-one years old. With four felonies and three state bids, Bravo chose to give his life to the streets.

It was night time and Bravo was with his right-hand man, Story, on their way to the corner store for a case of beers and a box of Dutch Masters.

"I heard Lil' Man got booked this morning, bro, you heard about that?" Bravo asked Story while they walked into the Ock store.

"Son got caught with a grip right in front of his building," Story said as his Cuban-link, 16-inch chain swung with every step.

Both men liked to wear jewelry to glorify their lifestyle, but to some, they were easy targets.

"Damn, they giving out three years for a grip, bro. Shit, getting caught with a gun is like getting knocked with a key of coke," Bravo said, paying for everything at the counter.

When both men turned around to leave, two gunmen ran up in the store with guns drawn.

Bloc, Bloc, Bloc, Bloc...

Boc, Boc, Boc, Boc, Boc...

When Story and Bravo's bodies hit the floor, Kazzy and Less were in their pockets looking for money. They took off all their jewelry.

Kazzy looked at the Ock behind the bulletproof glass who looked scared to death.

"Shhhh..." Kazzy placed a finger across his mouth before leaving.

***

Kazzy Loc and Less rode back to Webster projects in silence.

"You think this shit real?" Less said, looking at the two chains and two Rolex watches both men had on.

"We can sell them to my son from Hunters Point, he a African nigga," Kazzy Loc stated, trying get his money back up because he was down bad.

His main targets were Glock and all of his people. They already had a blueprint on who Glock dealt with, from Bankroll, Pop-Off, YG, and PG to his workers' traps all over the Bronx.

They weren't going to let up until they got him and his whole crew.

Chapter 14

Soundview, Bronx

Pop-Off's mom and brother lived in a house down the block from Soundview projects.

Last week, Pop-Off got his first advance check and gave his mom, Rebecca, $50,000 and his little brother $20,000, who had a seed on the way.

Rebecca was in the kitchen cooking dinner for Pop-Off, who was on his way home from doing a show in Boston. She was proud of her son coming up in the game. She was seeing so many niggas lose their lives in the streets to violence, and she was really proud of her son for making it.

Mims, her other son, was upstairs getting dressed for his night out on the town with his crew, going club hopping.

The doorbell rang, so she stopped stirring the ground beef and turned down the stove.

"Who is it?" Rebecca stated as she went to answer the door. It was so dark outside she couldn't even see who it was on her porch, and the light was broken.

When she opened the door a few inches, the door busted open and she was tackled to the ground. Paco covered her mouth so she couldn't scream as Black searched the house for the little brother who he saw come inside hours ago.

When Black went upstairs, he saw Mims in his room looking at himself. When he saw Black's gun he lifted his hands.

"The money is in the top drawer, man," he told Black.

With his gun still aimed at Mims, he made his way to the drawer and opened it, and saw a wad of money. When Black took the money, Mims ran off downstairs.

"Paco!" Black shouted, running out the room after him.

Downstairs, Paco had Mims at gunpoint while Rebecca was on the floor in tears. Black whipped Mims with the gun until his face was busted.

"Please, stop, if it's money you want, it's all in the kitchen cabinet inside of the Apple Jacks cereal box," she told Black, who looked like he was through pistol whipping.

Black's hands were bloody while going in the kitchen to look for the money, which he found easily.

"We gucci, son," Black stated, seeing all the money inside the green box.

Boc, Boc, Boc, Boc, Boc, Boc...

Paco killed Rebecca and Mims, giving them both head shots like it was a flu shot.

"Yoo, son, I ain't have Apple Jacks in dumb long, word to Mommy," Black stated, walking back to their stolen car.

"Let's go holler at Knight, this nigga blowing my phone up," Paco said, hopping in the old BMW they hijacked from a nigga at a stop sign hours ago.

***

Uptown, Bronx

"I called Paco ten times. Who the fuck I look like, his bitch?" Knight stated while driving with Kip Loc down Gun Hill Road.

"Bitches, with an *s*," Kip Loc stated while listening to a KJBalla mixtape.

"What, nigga? Better yet, fuck it, you ready, bro? This shit should be ready. This dreadhead be moving heavy pens of weed, and that's why I brought out the truck I rented. Son going to be loaded. He keeps everything in the basement of his liquor store. D Fatal Brim told me he is to split him and Glock wit' da bud. I miss that nigga, bro," Knight said, thinking about D Fatal Brim.

"He called me earlier and said he got your letter," Kip Loc said.

"That nigga call me twenty times a day and ask me the same shit. Where dem hoes at," Knight said, laughing, in D Fatal Brim's voice.

"Facts," Kip Loc said, knowing he was speaking truth.

The GM truck pulled over next to a fire zone because there was nowhere else to park.

"Let's be quick, 'cause I ain't trying to go to jail," Knight said, climbing out with his crew in tow.

The liquor store run by the Jamaicans was open to the public 24 hours. Everybody else was scared to keep their stores open past 10 pm, out of fear of being robbed.

When they entered, there was a tall, dark-skin Jamaican with long gray hair posted up. Once the dreadhead saw the guns, he pulled a shotgun from under the counter and let off two shots. Knight and Kip Loc took cover as the shotgun blasts shot through cases of liquor.

Bloc, Bloc, Bloc, Bloc, Bloc, Bloc...

Knight hit the dread in his neck twice, and his chest, making him crash into the wall, dropping the shotgun.

Two dreadheads in Rasta hats ran out from a side door blasting assault rifles like they were in the wild wild west.

Bloc, Bloc, Bloc...

Kip Loc hit one of the men in the dome.

"Boodclot!" the last gunman shouted.

Tat-tat-tat-tat-tat-tat-tat...

The last Jamaican was so focused on Kip Loc for just killing his brother, he didn't even see Knight sneak up on him.

Bloc, Bloc, Bloc...

Knight put three holes in the side of his head, leaving two long pieces of dreads on the floor.

Knight and Kip Loc went downstairs to see pounds of weed on a table and two neat stacks of money.

They had to make a couple of trips to load up the truck. Luckily, nobody saw them as they put a *we're closed* sign on the front door, while transporting everything inside the truck.

***

Queens, NY
1 Week Later

Queens had the best strip clubs in the city and tonight, Kip Loc was in his own small section with two crip niggas from his projects.

Kazzy Loc, Less, and Black texted him saying they were on their way in the next thirty minutes. Being twenty-one felt so good, he wanted to shout it out. He watched Spanish bitches do crazy tricks on the pole and strippers dance on customers all over the club. He already had 14 lap dances, and he smelled like perfume and sweat.

"I'ma go to the restroom, cuz," Trey said.

"Me too," Dawg stated, following Trey as Kip Loc sipped Henny out the bottle, his favorite drink.

Kip Loc had six bottles of Henny lined up on the table waiting to be opened, but he was waiting for his crew to arrive. As his favorite rapper, Dave East, played in the club speakers, he saw two big, black ass niggas approaching him with a light-skin nigga with a bald head.

When they entered his section, there was no talking. Kip Loc picked up a bottle of Henny and busted it on one of the big linebacker's heads.

Glock and the other goons started stabbing Kip Loc while holding him down, crushing him, hitting him over forty-five times. When Trey and Dawg got back and saw what was going on, they started fighting Glock and his guards until security rushed them.

Trey was stabbed twice in his heart. He and Kip Loc were dead on the scene before help arrived.

Chapter 15

New York City, NY

Summer Jamz was the livest concert of the year in the cut, and everybody and their family attended.

Bankroll and his crew were in the back section watching his homegirl he went to school with perform for the closing act, and she killed it! They were outside in a big field, shoulder to shoulder in a crowd full of people, drinking and smoking.

"Yo, son, I wish Glock would have came out," Mayo Da Don said, sipping lean out of a double foam cup.

"Glock in Jersey with the Paterson homies," Bankroll stated, following the crowd outside the gates. This was the only free time Bankroll had with his crew because shit had been so hacked dealing with Knight and his crew. Glock wanted Knight and his whole crew dead. Since killing Kip Loc, niggas been dying left and right in the Soundview section of the Bronx.

Less and Black were at Summer Jamz in the parking lot posted up with four other Mack Ballers. They were talking to females walking by looking like models.

"Yo, Blood, look at this," Less said, stiff tapping Black's arm.

"We about to ride on this nigga, brotty," Black said, seeing Bankroll and his crew walking through the lot.

Since Kip Loc's death, everybody had been on edge and hurt. Less wanted blood, and today was going to be that day. Less went to the trunk of the BMW coupe and pulled out a Draco. When Black saw what was about to go down, he pulled out his 40 cal, and his crew all did the same. They were running through the crowded parking lot like a wave.

Tat-tat-tat-tat-tat-tat-tat...
Boc, Boc, Boc, Boc, Boc...
Bloc, Bloc, Bloc, Bloc, Bloc....

Bankroll saw two of his men drop like flies. He spun around, firing at the gunmen who caught him slipping. The crowd was running in every direction as some people got hit in the crossfire. Less hit another one of Bankroll's soldiers with a dome shot.

Two police cars arrived and Less wasted no time emptying out the clip on the cop car. Bankroll aired out the other cop car, hitting one of the officers in his neck before running off. Going to prison wasn't in his plans today.

Black and Less blended into the crowd, making their way to their car. People were playing speed bumper trying to get out the lot as police cars rushed in twenty deep. Black and Less were the lucky two that made it out from their crew.

***

Brooklyn, NY

Katty just got done working the pole in Club Sky's, which was an upscale strip club in Brooklyn.

Tonight, she made $9,000, and it was one young nigga in the club who was tossing all blue faces when she was dancing. He was her number one supporter tonight and the main reason why she was leaving with a couple of stacks.

Katty was in the dressing room by herself getting dressed. She loved looking at her body as she stood in the mirror making her ass clap. She opened her locker and grabbed her designer bag and pulled out her jeans, blouse, and heels. When she closed her locker, she saw the man who was spending all of his money on her.

"You're not allowed to be down here, fucking creep," Katty said, nervous, covering her boobs thinking he was going to try to rape her, because she was raped twice.

YG laughed and pulled out a 9mm with a silencer attached to it.

"Where can I find Paco, ma? I'll walk right upstairs never looking back if you tell me, sexy," YG stated, hoping nobody would come downstairs, but all the women were working the floor.

"Nigga, what the fuck I look like? Suck my dick!" Katty shouted, spitting in his face, then kicking him in his balls, trying to get inside her locker where her gun was at.

Paco always made her and Hasley carry weapons for their own protection. When she got her locker open, YG grabbed her by her hair, slamming her to the floor.

"You stuck-up bitch!" YG yelled, in pain from her kicking him in his balls.

PSST, PSST, PSST, PSST...

YG shot her in her beautiful face, then left, heading out the side exit in the hallway. Two dancers came downstairs and started screaming when they saw Katty's dead body in a pool of blood.

***

161st, Bronx
Two Days Later

The courthouse was filled with lawyers, court clerks, and criminals who were fighting cases. Inmates were also coming from local precincts and Rikers Island Jail for their court dates.

PG was waiting to see the judge for the gun charge he was out on bail for. PG hated courts, cuffs, cops, and jails, but he knew it was a part of the lifestyle he chose.

His lawyer was nowhere to be found when his name was called, but he went in front of the judge anyway.

"Judge, Mr. Andullah's lawyer is not here today. I believe we should reschedule until next week," the DA told the judge.

"I agree, next week it is," the judge said, banging his gavel.

PG turned and walked out of the courtroom, wondering why his lawyer didn't call him to let him know he wasn't showing up.

***

Less waited on the side of the courthouse smoking a cigarette, seeing PG walk by without a care in the world, on his phone. Less went in the courthouse to pay for two new tickets he got for speeding, but when he saw PG going inside a courtroom, he went to get his gun and waited on him.

When PG crossed the street, shots started to ring out with one hitting his upper back.

"Ahhhhhh... fuck!" PG said, turning back to see Less in a hoodie trying to hunt him down.

PG ran down the street, sliding over cars while ducking bullets. Less saw PG was too far down the block, and he ran off before the police came.

Chapter 16

Miami, FL
One Month Later

Pop-Off was in the studio in Miami recording his new album *Caged In*, which was a smash hit.

Dej Jamz was backing his movement and album. This was Pop-Off's first time in Miami and he was loving the club scenes, but he knew he had to focus on his album.

Losing his mom and little brother was heavy on his heart and mind. He needed to come to Miami to clear his head and get away from the crazy shit. He brought two niggas from Soundview projects down to Miami with him.

"What we doing tonight, son?" Wall said as he rolled a blunt full of loud.

"It's whatever y'all want to do," Pop-Off said, coming out the booth grabbing a bottle of Moët from the table.

When Pop-Off sat down next to Wall, the studio door flew open and two gunmen in ski masks ran inside with assault rifles.

Tat-tat-tat-tat-tat-tat-tat-tat-tat-tat-tat-tat-tat-tat-tat...

Knight and Kazzy Loc killed everybody in the studio except Pop-Off, who was hiding behind a couch.

"Pop-Off, come out, bro, where you going to go?" Knight stated, seeing Pop-Off standing up, shaking.

Pop-Off couldn't believe niggas came to Miami to get him. He had no connections to any guns in Miami, so he was rolling with knives.

Tat-tat-tat-tat-tat-tat-tat-tat....

Pop-Off's body slammed into the wall and he collapsed on the floor.

Kazzy Loc and Knight walked out towards the front where they had three people hogtied. They shot everybody in the head before they made it outside.

"Damn, bro, that Cuban bitch was fire. We ain't have to kill her, cuz," Kazzy Loc said.

"Nigga, shut up, you tryna get niggas booked out here," Knight said, climbing in the truck.

Knight and Kazzy took a trip to Miami to meet up with a Puerto Rican chick they knew from the projects. She had a boyfriend who was getting money, and she had Knight and Kazzy Loc rob him.

The Puerto Rican chick thought she was getting a cut, but instead, she received a 223 bullet to the head after the robbery.

Later that night, Knight and Kazzy both went out to a strip club called G Five and saw Pop-Off in the VIP booth. Since that night, they'd been tailing him, and now it was time to go back to New York.

***

Mount Vernon, NY
Four Days Later

"Uhmmmmm, fuck," LaLa moaned while Kazzy Loc fucked her tight pussy. She was throwing her ass back, making it clap on his dick.

Kazzy grabbed a hand full of her hair and rammed himself deep into her juicy sex. The two had been in the hotel for two hours fucking, smoking, and drinking. They met at the basketball courts, and she was feeling Kazzy. He was moving like a boss type nigga.

Her pussy was so good, Kazzy Loc had to pull out before he shot his load in her. LaLa wanted to take his dick for a ride, so she straddled him. LaLa let his dick sink into her pussy while she lowered herself.

"Oh my god, Jamel," she moaned, calling him another nigga's name, but her pussy was so good, he ain't care as he fucked her hard and rough.

He had her screaming at the top of her lungs as he fucked her core.

A half an hour later, they were leaving the hotel on their way to the state park near River Park Towers, overlooking the Hudson River.

"Tell me more about yourself. I know you got mad bitches," she said, sounding jealous.

"I do, but I'm tryna make you number one," he said, making her smile.

Kazzy pulled into the dark park in an area next to the Hudson River.

"This is so nice. I never been over here. Let's chill on the hood, I got a surprise for you," LaLa said, getting out of the car, looking at the stars and water.

When Kazzy leaned on his car hood, LaLa pulled his pants down and started sucking his dick. Her mouth game was so crazy, he had tears in his eyes while she deepthroated him using her lips and tongue. Kazzy Loc couldn't hold himself as he came in her mouth. She continued to suck his dick until he went limp, then she spit it out.

"You could have told me you were cumming. I don't swallow."

"Why suck dick if you don't swallow?" Kazzy Loc asked while pulling up his pants.

"It tastes nasty," she said, standing up holding his hand like they were a couple now because she sucked his dick.

They went to stare into the water with LaLa in front of him. Kazzy had his hands around her waist behind her.

"Where do you see yourself in five years?" she asked.

"Not where you're about to go," Kazzy Loc said, backing up.

"What?" she said, turning around, not understanding what he meant. When she saw the gun in her face, her eyes bucked.

Boc, Boc...

Kazzy Loc shot her between her eyes and tossed her body in the dark river, hearing the loud splash. When he saw LaLa, it was Black who told him she was the one who set him and Less up in Mott Haven, but they were still unaware she was YG and PG's sister.

Chapter 17

Fordham University, BX

Knight was waiting for BeBe, his little sister, to come out of class so he could spend some time with her.

While he was waiting, a short, thick, beautiful, blonde-haired white woman bumped into Knight.

"Oh, excuse me," she said, almost knocking his phone out his hand.

When he saw how sexy she was, he paused, looking into her colorful eyes, feeling that fatal attraction.

"I didn't see you, but where are you headed? Can I walk you?" Knight asked while she looked at his big rope chain and Rolex watch.

"Yes, I don't mind. Do you go to school here? I've never seen you around and this school is not so big." She started walking through the hallways.

"I don't, but my sister, BeBe, goes here. I'm just coming to pick her up," Knight stated.

"Oh, I see. What's your name?"

"Knight, how about you?"

"Mila," she stated.

"You got swag for a white chick," he said, looking at her designer outfit.

"I'm half Puerto Rican, I just look white," Mila said, giving him a look, letting him know he should not judge a book by its cover.

"You still beautiful."

"Thank you, Mr., you're not too bad yourself," Mila added.

"What are you in school for?"

"To become a DA, so I'm on my last year to get my criminal justice degree," she replied, stopping at her class door while students went in to take their seats.

"How about you take my number and call me?" Knight said, and she agreed. After he gave her his number, he went back to holler at his sister to see if she was ready.

***

BeBe was waiting by her class door, calling Knight to see where he was at. She was looking good in her low-cut jeans and short top, showing off her toned stomach. She was medium height and brown skinned, with long hair she placed in a ponytail. BeBe could have been a model, but her dreams were to open businesses for young black people. At nineteen years old, she had her mind in the right place, unlike her brothers, who were running the streets.

"There you go. Oh my god, can we please leave?" BeBe said, seeing Knight stroll down the hall as if he went to school there.

"I was waiting on you," he said, walking out the school.

"Oh, shit, I forgot my tablet," BeBe said, turning around to go inside the school.

Across the street, Knight saw Glock coming out of a lawyer's office. They locked eyes, both men ready to shoot it out, but there were too many people walking up and down the block. NYPD cops were also parked at the corner watching the heavy traffic on the busy main street.

Glock gave him a head nod before he climbed in an Uber, pulling off. Knight laughed as BeBe came out the school.

"Let's go shopping, baller," BeBe said with excitement in her voice.

"Shopping, what the fuck I look like? I called you so we can go out for lunch," he said, climbing in his car.

"Lunch? Broke ass nigga, I don't want no lunch. I want some money," BeBe said, leaning back in the Benz's leather seats.

"You need a job."

"Whatever," she replied, turning up the Fabolous and Jada album.

They went to a city island to enjoy a seafood meal and a view of the ocean while talking, laughing, and reminiscing about when they were kids.

***

East Burnside, BX

Knocks was a big-time drug dealer in his hood. He was busting down keys and selling grams to niggas in the hood. His plug was Glock, and every week he was going twenty or more bricks of raw coke, no cut on it.

It was a late night and he was in the lobby of his apartment building with two other niggas he grew up with.

"You heard what happened to Pop-Off in Miami?" Steven asked while rolling up a blunt of loud.

"I heard them Haitian niggas out there ran up in the studio," Marky said, sitting on the stairs repeating what he'd been hearing in the streets.

"Man, y'all niggas know who jacked them niggas, son," Knocks stated, texting one of his bitches, telling her to come through.

"Who you think did it, bro?" Steven said, seeing the front door open.

Marky was the first to reach for his gun when he saw the two gunmen with long pistols enter the lobby.

Bloc, Bloc, Bloc...

Marky's body jerked before collapsing on the stairs. Steven took two shots to the head. Knocks looked as if he saw a ghost.

"Go inside," Kazzy Loc said, grabbing Knocks by his collar, pushing him toward the first apartment on his left.

Kazzy Loc and Paco were told by a close friend of Knocks' that he kept money and his drugs in the same crib like a dummy. Knocks went inside the apartment to see two of his young birds sleeping on the couch, drunk off liquor. Paco shot both of the youngsters in the head.

"We want the money and the drugs, son," Kazzy Loc said, stopping in the living room.

"The money is in the backroom AC in the window, and the work is in the shoe boxes under the bed, bro. I don't want no problems, I respect y'all movement, Blood," Knocks said, thinking they were Bloods because he heard the niggas running around jacking niggas in the BX were Bloods.

"Nigga, watch your mouth, I'm cripping," Kazzy Loc said while Paco was in the back loading up a duffle bag he found in Knocks' closet.

"My bad, no disrespect, big homie."

"Where is Glock?" Kazzy asked.

"Soundview, he's always in the front," Knocks stated, talking fast, hoping he was clear. "His baby mother lives in Gun Hill, a bad bitch named Olivia," Knocks added.

"We litty, son was holding somethin' lit, bro," Paco stated, coming out the back with a heavy duffle bag.

"I—" *Bloc, Bloc, Bloc, Bloc, Bloc...*

Kazzy hit Knocks five times, cutting off his sentence as Knocks' body slammed into the carpet.

Chapter 18

Hunts Point, BX

Mrs. Woodberry just got off work from her job as a CO on The Boat, which was a small county holdover jail on a real boat in the middle of the Hudson River. The Boat wasn't dangerous like the Rikers Island Jail in Queens, but it was close.

Mrs. Woodberry was a short older woman who lived in a nice section of the Bronx with her husband. She was the aunty of Black, whom she loved dearly. He was her favorite nephew. The other night, Black took her and her husband to a dinner in the city, and they all had a good time. Approaching her new Audi SUV, she saw her two front tires were slashed.

"What the hell!" she shouted, seeing someone cut her tires.

She looked around to see if any of her co-workers were around so she could get some help. A Charger pulled up with tints from behind her, and she waved them down, hoping to get a lift across town.

"Do you think I can get a ride across town? I have gas money," she stated while the driver rolled his window down.

When Mrs. Woodberry saw the young man's face, it looked familiar, but she couldn't figure it out.

The driver lifted a gun and shot her four times in her heart before pulling off.

**

YG drove away from the crime scene with a smirk, looking in his rearview mirror seeing Black's aunty on the ground bleeding out. The other day, YG was tailing Black and he saw him interacting with her as if she was family.

When YG got a good look at her, it hit him she was the woman who worked on The Boat. YG got locked up twice and went to The Boat, where he saw Mrs. Woodberry. She had the biggest ass outta all the female COs, so it was hard for him to forget who she was.

YG and PG had been trying to get up with Black, Less, Paco, Knight, or Kazzy, but it'd been hard because they all moved like ninjas. Since losing LaLa, the brothers had been on bullshit, killing everything in sight to get to their ops.

***

46th Precinct, Bronx

Detective Woodberry sat behind her desk looking at a caseload of robberies and killings, all with the same motives. She was a forty-year-old black NYPD detective in the Bronx, 46th precinct, with a good resume. At forty, she looked amazing, with brown skin and a toned, perfect body from daily exercises, and she had beautiful facial features.

She was the mother of Black and her younger son, Blu. Being a single mother was hard, but she tried her best and did a damn good job in her books. She knew both of her children were in the streets and both were into gang activity.

The past few months, she'd been working hard on investigating a couple of murders of local drug dealers. She clicked on her computer mouse and stared at the picture of a man who was number one on every detective's hit list: Knight.

Detective Woodberry had known Knight since he was a little baby. She lived in the same building as him for years, and she knew how close Black and Knight were. She knew there was no strong evidence on Knight, but their informants couldn't keep his name out their mouths.

The shit she was hearing, she couldn't believe a good kid like Knight would do, or Kazzy. She knew them both since they were babies running around MillBrook projects.

"Mrs. Woodberry, you may want to check this out. It's fresh from the 49th precinct," a cop who worked on homicide with her said, walking in her office with a laptop. "Wait until you see this."

When he started clicking through the gruesome photos of her sister laying on the floor covered in her own blood, she started crying. The cop excused himself, not knowing Woodberry knew who the dead woman was.

Det. Woodberry cried for over ten minutes because her sister was a good person. She treated everybody with love and care. She couldn't think of one person who would want to do anything to her sister at all.

Det. Woodberry left her office to get the evidence from the 49th precinct so she could take the case, because this was personal.

***

Fordham, Bronx

The Salsa Con Fuego Lounge was jumping tonight on Reggaeton Friday. Spanish chicks were dancing everywhere in their best outfits while the men picked and chose who they wanted to leave with.

Black and Paco were out and about tonight, drinking and getting over their losses. Paco was hurt about Katty's death, and Black was upset about his aunty, who was found dead in Hunts Point.

The crew was almost back on their feet. The Knocks lick they split with everybody as always, so now they were selling weight and plotting the next victim.

"I'ma hit the dance floor and get my salsa on, bro. I'll be back," Paco said, leaving Black at the bar. Seeing his boy drink so much made Paco's heart go out to him.

"You look like you can use some company," a sexy bartender said, wiping down the counter.

"It's better to be alone, than in the wrong company," Black said, drinking, paying the Dominican eye candy no mind. He'd been seeing dudes holler at the bartender all night, but she respectfully curved all of them.

"It depends on the company," she said, placing a new glass of Henny in front of him.

"You don't know how to leave a nigga alone and let him vent, I see," he said, looking into her nice, soft eyes.

"Nope... I'm from da Bronx, papi, you know how we do," she said, walking off to help another customer.

Black saw how phat her ass was in her black jeans and almost choked. He found out her name was Kavita and she just got out of an abusive relationship. Most of the night, they spent getting to know each other, which led to another thing. They ended up having sex in the club bathroom, and that led to a night at Black's new crib he had in Williamsburg.

Kavita's pussy was so good, Black didn't want her to leave. He ended up cooking her breakfast in bed and took her on a fun-filled day of shopping and sightseeing in Times Square. Black was surprised they had so much in common and they both had similar upbringings.

Chapter 19

Parkchester, Bronx

Yvette was sitting in her room cleaning up and picking up Kazzy's clothes. This was her off day from work, so she normally cleaned up around the house and spent time with Kazzy.

Some papers fell out of Kazzy's pants pocket, so she picked them up and read them. She was very respectful when it came to her man's privacy, but lately, since her brother died, Kazzy had been acting weird.

She was reading the receipts from Miami dated back to the same day her brother was murdered. When she dug deeper into his pants, she found a card with the address to the studio where Pop-Off, her brother, was killed.

Yvette sat down in deep thought, because she knew what kind of man Kazzy was. She knew Pop-Off was in the streets beefing with niggas, because he told her.

Kazzy was never introduced to Yvette's brother and she never told her brother about Kazzy. Everything wasn't adding up. Kazzy would have told her if he was going to Miami for any reason. Yvette searched for more clues for over an hour, like she was a detective.

***

Castle Hill, Bronx

Bankroll's new girlfriend, Yasmain, was a thick, beautiful Dominican woman who worked in a salon. Yasmain was in the back washing one of her client's hair in the sink. Her client was the last one of the day, which she was thankful for because she was tired and her feet and hands were hurting.

"You're done, girl, I know you about to hit the stage and get it how you live," Yasmain said, washing her hands, ready to leave.

"Thank you, gurl, you came through for a bitch today," her customer said, about to let her hair air dry.

"Anytime, but let's get the fuck outta here, my man waiting on me," Yasmain said, grabbing her purse out the back room.

When she came out the back, she saw two men with big guns, and one of the guns was pointed at her customer's temple.

"This is a nice little shop. You own this joint?" Kazzy asked, walking around touching her products.

"I'm a woman, you should be ashamed of yourself," Yasmain stated, making Less laugh while pressing his gun to her client's head.

"Bitch, we a new breed of killers out here, this ain't the fucking 1960s. Now, let's get down to the point. Where can I find your boyfriend?" Kazzy asked, standing face to face with her.

Last week, Kazzy picked up Yvette from Yasmain's hair salon and saw Bankroll waiting for her in the front of the shop. Since then, Kazzy had been coming to the shop at the same time before closing to peep Bankroll's routines. Tonight, Bankroll was out of town getting money in Rochester with his cousin.

"I don't know who you're talking about, and I'm not scared of you because you got a gun. I'm from Castle Hill projects, papi," Yasmain said, sounding tough.

Kazzy gave Less a slight head nod, and Less blew her client's head off her shoulders. Yasmain thought the two men were talking, but now they made her a true believer.

"Shall we start over?" Kazzy asked, putting his gun to her forehead, seeing sweat drop onto his pistol.

"Ok, I know his cousin is a big-time drug dealer in Rochester. His name is Peanut. Bankroll got a lot of family up there, he up there now," she said, feeling like she just crossed her man, but she knew her life was more valuable.

"That's all you have for us?" Less asked.

"Uhmmm." She nodded.

Boc, Boc, Boc, Boc, Boc...

Blood from her head shot splattered everywhere.

"Why the fuck you always do that?" Less said, wiping the blood off his lip.

"Do what?" Kazzy said, walking out.

"Nigga, give me a warning. I was standing right there. What if you would have missed her and shot me?" Less stated.

"You would have been a dead motherfucker," Kazzy stated, laughing.

Chapter 20

Uptown BX

Black never wanted no female as bad as he wanted Kavita today. Her dress and heels were across the room on the floor.

They both closed their eyes and got loud into each other, letting the strong passion they shared erupt through their tongues. Black started sucking on her left nipple, making her moan loudly.

"Shhhhiiiitttt..." Kavita moaned, grabbing his head. Kavita was normally quiet during her lovemaking, but Black made her turn up a notch.

She started breathing shallow when he went farther down south, licking all over her stomach until he got to her neatly shaved peach. Kavita spread her legs open while he sucked on her clit, digging his face into her waterfall.

"Ohhhh my god, Black," she moaned, lifting her hips up off the bed, grinding her pussy onto his face.

Before she was about to cum, he stopped, getting her upset, but when he climbed between her legs and went inside of her, loosening up her little coochie, she went crazy.

"Ohhh, yesss!" she screamed at the top of her lungs.

Black pushed her legs back as far as they would go, making her wrap her ankles around his neck. She came within two minutes, feeling him beat her walls down while making passionate love to her. While Black was in mid-stroke, his iPhone started ringing non-stop. Knowing it had to be important, he pulled out.

"No the fuck you didn't just do that," Kavita said with a look of evil in her eyes.

Black paid her no mind. Climbing out the bed to go to his phone on his dresser, he saw it was his mom, who never called him.

"Right now, Mom... Ok."

Kavita heard a woman yelling on the phone from across the room, so whatever it was, she knew sex was over for the night. This night turned from the best day to the worst in a matter of minutes.

"Can you please stay here while I go meet my mom? I'll be right back," he asked, getting dressed.

"No, I'm coming," Kavita said, getting dressed, not taking no for an answer.

***

138th, Bronx

Detective Woodberry was at a 24-hour diner waiting on her son to find out what was really going on, because she knew Black wasn't innocent. If Kazzy was into something, then she knew the whole crew was, everybody from Black, Less, Paco, and Knight. She was saddened when she heard about Kip's death. He was her favorite, so respectful.

She saw Black and a pretty chick walk in the diner. Before she could even say hi, the woman with Black hugged her, somewhat surprising her.

"Hey, I'm Kavita, Black's girlfriend," Kavita said, already claiming wifey status.

"I'm his mother, nice to meet you. I didn't know my son had a girlfriend, but you're beautiful."

"Thank you, Black hasn't mentioned you yet, but I see you're a cop," Kavita said, looking at her police badge on her waist and her work gun poking out her holster.

"Yep, I'm a cop. How about you, what do you do for a living?" she replied.

"Kavita, can you give me and my mom a few minutes real quick?" Black asked, kissing her on her lips.

"Ok, no problem, nice to meet you," Kavita said, walking off.

"She seems like a sweet girl, the perfect hustler's wife," his mom said, being sarcastic.

"Come on, Mom, please don't start this."

"Don't start what, Brock?" she said, calling him by his real name.

"Nothing, Mom, how you doing? You look great," Black said, looking at her flawless skin.

"What is going on, Black? And don't bullshit a bullshitter. I had this chick named Yvette come to the precinct telling me Kazzy killed her brother, Pop-Off."

"What?" Black said, playing dumb.

"Brock, she is willing to confess to a couple of unsolved murders. I know you're not an angel and those are your friends, but I'm your mother. Let me help you."

"Mom, there is nothing to help. You're a cop, I'm on the streets, we're on different fields. I sit back and watch your people kill my people every day and get acquitted for it."

"Let me make myself clear to you, little boy. You think you're a man because you're out here busting your gun, selling poison, killing innocent people? That makes you a fucking coward. My people aren't color. I became a cop to show kids, my kids, you, people, that you can be a Black woman and protect and serve. I'm here to protect our communities, not destroy," she said firmly.

"Mom, I ain't come to argue, thanks for telling me," he said, standing to leave.

"If you don't sit your black ass down, I will make a movie outta you," she said.

Black sat down, knowing how crazy his mother was.

"You know why I still live in the projects?" she asked him.

"No, why?"

"Because I want to show people that I will never forget where I came from. Don't let greed or the streets override your true self. You're a good kid. I know it because I raised you. All that street stuff and Blood stuff is just a phase. You're not a man yet until you grow from it, trust me," she said, getting up to leave.

When his mom left, he thought about everything she just said before getting up to leave himself.

* * *

Black's mind was spinning with thoughts as he drove through Mott Haven projects on his way back home. Kavita was talking the whole time, but Black was unable to hear one word because he drowned her out with the rap music playing.

Black had to get up with Kazzy Loc first thing in the morning to tell him about Yvette. Black met her a couple of times and he always got good vibes from her.

Hearing she was Pop-Off's sister was new to him. He wondered if Kazzy Loc knew, but there was no question something had to give soon or everybody could be in jail with D Fatal Brim.

It was almost midnight and niggas were posted up all over the block. When he was about to stop at a stop sign, bullets shattered his car windows. Black pushed Kavita's head down so she wouldn't get hit as bullets came from everywhere. He pulled off, getting a quick glimpse of YG and PG with four other shooters.

He was able to make it down the street where he was safe. Kavita looked like she just escaped from Hell fighting the devil, making Black laugh. When she saw Black laugh, she knew she was feeling another crazy nigga.

Chapter 21

Long Island, NY

Knight and his crew all posted up inside the Tahoe SUV watching the mansion down the street. Three guards were posted up outside early in the morning watching their boss's wife fix up her garden.

"Yo, Paco, how you hear about this nigga?" Kazzy Loc asked from the backseat, staring at the Puerto Rican men.

"His bitch is bad, boy, that's a fact." Less stared at Manganiello's beautiful wife, who was wearing a sundress with her hair in a bun.

"Y'all gonna ask questions or we about to go up in here and do?" Paco asked everybody while he loaded up on his MackII, placing a silencer on the barrel.

This was the first mission the crew went on together, ever. Paco knew they needed all the manpower for the Puerto Rican kingpin whose name was heavy all over Puerto Rico and New York.

"How many you think inside?" Knight asked, trying to plot everything out before running up in there on some wild man shit.

"Maybe four or five, I'm not really sure, that's why I think we should split up. It's a back entrance through the backdoor." Paco knew it was best to split up.

"That's smart," Black stated, thinking of if this was the perfect time to tell Kazzy his wifey was a rat.

"You good, bro? Word to mother, son, you been acting funny these last couple of days." Kazzy was looking behind him talking to Black.

"I'ma holler at you later, fam, we gotta talk," Black stated.

"Say that," Kazzy replied.

"I think we should make our move now," Paco said, getting out the truck pulling his mask over his face, sneaking across the street.

It was a nice sunny morning outside for killing, and they planned to do just that today. The guards were all so busy looking at their boss's wife, Salma, bent over showing her nice, perfect apple bottom, they didn't see the attack.

Psst, Psst, Psst, Psst, Psst, Psst, Psst, Psst, Psst, Psst, Psst, Psst, Psst, Psst, Psst...

The guards and Salma were all dead in a matter of seconds. Paco, Less, and Knight went through the front while Black and Kazzy went through the back. Creeping through the front door, a man was standing up on the phone with his back towards them.

PSST, PSST, PSST, PSST...

The security guard's body fell hard, making a loud thump.

"What the fuck is going—aye!" Another guard came out the living room area around the corner.

Before the guard could reach for his gun, his body was filled with hollow tips, putting air holes in his body. Knight saw Black and Kazzy Loc walk out from the back area.

"There was only one back there. We gonna head up top," Kazzy Loc stated, going up the stairs to the second level while the other crew went downstairs, which was a pool area, gym, and indoor bathhouse.

"Damn, nigga, you gonna push me down the stairs?" Knight told Less, who was in his back.

"Nigga, you in my way," Less shot back.

"Shhhhh..." Paco whispered as they saw a man swimming laps up and down the indoor pool.

Bloc, Bloc...

The shots came from a guard who was sitting behind the doorway. When he saw the men creep downstairs, he fired, having the ups on them but missing due to his lazy eye.

PSST, PSST, PSST, PSST, PSST, PSST...

The guard's body flew into the wall, holding him up as he collapsed on the floor.

Manganiello stopped swimming after hearing all the commotion. He took off his goggles and looked at the three gentlemen standing in front of him.

"Paco..." Manganiello said in a surprised voice, shocked to see his godson.

"You thought I would never find out, Godfather?"

"Paco, this is unacceptable, your uncle was a snake. He bit the hand that fed him. That's what happens when someone does wrong in the game, they pay with their life. I would like to finish my last lap," Manganiello said, swimming off.

"That nigga gangsta, son. You just gonna stand there and let him stunt on you like that? I knew you was soft. It's always you pretty boy niggas," Less started shit.

When Manganiello climbed out the pool, Paco shot him nine times in the chest, going into overkill mode. Manganiello's body fell into the pool, turning the water red. Paco then pushed Less into the bloody water, knowing he couldn't swim.

"You bloody fo' real now, son," Paco said laughing, seeing Less about to drown, but Knight helped him out the pool while Paco went upstairs.

Once back upstairs, Paco saw Black and Kazzy standing there with four designer suitcases. He saw the two men going back and forth as if they were in a heated argument.

"Nigga, why would you wait this long to tell me? That's goofy, she could have gotten all of us knocked off, B!" Kazzy shouted.

"That's your bitch. You should have known who sister she was, you dumb ass nigga," Black matched his tone, not backing down.

"Nah, son, Yvette a rat and this clown knew all along." Kazzy was mad at Black, but really at himself.

"Watch your mouth." Black pointed in Kazzy's face.

"Or what?" Kazzy was now ready to fight.

"Y'all niggas wilding, we need to go take care of that later," Paco said, glad they found the stash.

Everybody left the mansion without saying another word to each other. At Black's crib, they split everything and went their separate ways.

***

181ˢᵗ Rye Ave, Bronx
Two Days Later

Yvette was on her way to meet Detective Woodberry to give her some details and info she found on Kazzy, when she saw him standing in front of her car with flowers.

"Hey, you," she said, putting on a fake smile.

"These for you, love. Where you going?"

"Huhh... I'm going to work, baby."

"At this time?" Kazzy caught her in her lie.

"I've been doing doubles, but I have to go." She got a little nervous, feeling something about his presence was off.

"Why did you do it?" Kazzy asked, pulling out a gun, seeing her start crying. Kazzy Loc didn't wanna hear her reply. He shot her in the head then jogged off.

Chapter 22

Brooklyn, NY
One Week Later

Detective Woodberry just left the condo of her man, who she'd been dealing with for a couple months. He wasn't too sexy by far, but he had a good heart and treated her like a queen. The sex was always on point, and her little peach was sore from the long night of rough, passionate sex.

He knew she was a cop and that didn't bother him at all, he was into real estate. She never met a man like Fats before, and she hoped it would soon go further than just sex.

On her way back home, she thought about the news of Yvette's death outside of her apartment. One thing Detective Woodberry learned in all her time of being a cop, was whenever someone shot a victim in the head, it was personal.

There was no doubt in her mind who was behind the murder, but there was nothing she planned to do about it except place the case in the cold case files in the basement.

***

Park Ave, Bronx

Kavita was taking her mom food shopping to pick up a couple of things since she was too old to drive or go shopping alone. Inside the grocery store, Kavita walked into the chips and soda aisle and saw the last person she wanted to see, her ex-boyfriend.

Kavita's mom was deaf and in an electric wheelchair, so she wasn't paying anybody no mind.

"Kavita, you look good, baby girl," Bankroll said smiling.

"Thanks, Bankroll, take care." She tried to walk past him with her mom in front of her.

"I see you found a new nigga." Bankroll saw the look on her face and wanted to laugh.

"Yeah, and he don't beat the shit out of me and put me in the hospital. Now, please, get the fuck out my face." Kavita walked off, ready to leave. She'd rather shop somewhere else than be in the same area as Bankroll.

In her relationship with Bankroll, all he did was abuse her and cheat on her with no chill button. Just seeing his face brought back old memories.

Outside, she helped her mom into her Range, unaware of Bankroll sneaking up behind her.

"You chose the wrong side."

"What? Nigga, fuck you," she spat back at Bankroll before he pulled his handgun out his lower back, putting two holes in her forehead.

Bankroll then shot her mom three times in her chest with no mercy for the elder. A couple of days ago, one of Bankroll's homie's folks said his ex-girlfriend was fucking with one of them Mill Brook niggas.

Upset was an understatement. Bankroll was on fire because he was still in love with her.

***

White Plains, NY
One Month Later

Knight was at the Greyhound bus station on his way to VA to go check his uncle Slim who had just gotten out of the feds last week from serving a five-year bid of a twenty-year sentence. His uncle was able to get time back and came home early from his drug charge.

He got in touch with Knight telling him to come to VA, and he agreed. Knight needed a vacation from the Bronx. Shit was on fire, and niggas were getting arrested left and right by the feds and state.

The last robbery the crew did, everybody received a nice amount of money. Knight gave all his drugs to Kazzy, who would sell them while Knight went to VA.

***

Richmond, VA

Knight got off the bus the next morning, his ass, back, and body stiff and aching from the ride.

"Nephew, what's up," Uncle Slim said, approaching Knight, hugging him. Uncle Slim was a tall, skinny nigga with braids who was from the Bronx, but years ago, he moved out to VA to get money.

"Damn, Unc, you let that jail shit wash you up," Knight said, looking at his gray beard.

"Nah, that's from stressing, kid. Come on, head to my place." Uncle Slim hopped in a rare luxury car. "You look like one of these country niggas with them dirty ass dreads and that damn grill in your mouth. Since when they started doing that in New York again?" Uncle Slim asked, driving through the city part of Richmond.

"I am Bronx, nigga. I'm trendsetting," Knight stated.

"I hear you, but what you been doing out there?"

"On money, you know how I do," Knight said, looking out the window.

"I got some shit going on here. I got shit for the low, everything from coke to dog food," Uncle Slim replied.

"Oh yeah?"

"I'ma put you on, but first I want to show you how I'm doing out here. Niggas out here getting a bag foreal. I heard you and your brothers are up top robbing everything moving. I heard Kip passed."

"Yeah, they got little bro, but I'ma make sure they pay," Knight stated seriously.

"Facts," Uncle Slim stated, catching up with his nephew.

Romell Tukes

Chapter 23

MDC Brooklyn, NY
One Month Later

D Fatal Brim just got off the day room phone with his lawyer who was gathering up evidence, statements on his behalf, and anything he could use to stand trial with. It was 9 am and most of the prisoners were sleeping, exercising, or just getting up, making a cup of coffee to start their day.

The feds had been snatching up a lot of gang members from the Bronx and placing them in the MDC building. Niggas was telling him stories about how Kazzy Loc, Black, Less, and Paco had the streets. Plus, the Bronx had been heavy on the news for the past couple of months. Bodies were dropping everywhere.

This was his morning routine, wake up at 6 am, drink some coffee, and exercise in his cell because niggas loved body watching on the unit. He would then use the computer, take a shower, make a call, then watch the news.

He was well respected in the joint. The whole jail knew of his case and street status as a gangsta, so nobody even thought about trying him.

A corrections officer called him for a visit. He had a clue who it was pulling up.

"You about to go dance with the stars, Blood?" one of his homies asked, sitting in a chair next to him watching the news on the TV.

"Facts, soon. Here, hold that until I come back, skrap," D Fatal Brim said, reaching into his boxers pulling out a big, long, sharp knife.

"Aight."

***

On the visit, D Fatal Brim smiled when he saw Less sitting with a bad Puerto Rican bitch. He knew today was going to be a good day.

D Fatal Brim embraced Less then he kissed the Puerto Rican chick in the mouth, tonguing her down. She passed him three loonies full of dope, mouth to mouth. The transaction was so smooth, nobody would suspect a thing.

"I'ma leave you two alone, papi. I'll be back in for the next hour," the woman stated, getting up to leave.

"Damn, where you find her at?" D Fatal Brim stared at the way her big ass sat in her jeans.

"West Bronx, a bitch will do anything for a couple of racks, but she all yours, son," Less stated, knowing she was gonna be the talk of the jail.

"Good looks, son, really though, but what's poppin' out there, skrap? Y'all niggas names is ringing in here, facts of life, son." D Fatal Brim hoped his brother was smarter than him.

"Since Kip died, we been robbing anybody who was close to Glock." Less hated saying Glock's name because he couldn't help but think about Kip and how they caught him slipping.

"Where's Knight?" D Fatal Brim changed the subject because hearing Kip's name brought grief to his heart. He saw Kip on the news the next morning after the night he was killed, and it took a toll on him.

"He in VA trying to open up something with his uncle who just came home from prison down south," Less replied.

"Ok, how's everybody? This nigga Paco just sent me $10,000 and some pies."

"That's what's up, Blood. I ain't seen that nigga in weeks, bro," Less said.

"I start trial in a couple of months or at the latest, next year."

"We need you home. Shit ain't the same without you," Less said, being honest.

"I know. I can't front, I used to have shit litty out there," D Fatal Brim boasted.

"Word to mother, B," Less said laughing, thinking of all the crazy shit they used to do.

They finished the hour visit and then D Fatal Brim did an hour visit with the Puerto Rican chick, who let him grab on her ass and pussy whenever the guards weren't watching them closely.

***

Diamond District, New York City

Paco was in an upscale jewelry store looking at Cuban-link chains and watches.

"Excuse me, sir, is that your Audi outside?" a beautiful light-skin woman asked, tapping his shoulder.

When Paco saw how she looked, he almost fumbled over his words. He could tell she was Colombian, but she was eye candy.

"Yes, no, maybe?" she stated, seeing he was zoned out.

"Yeah, it's mine. You need me to move it?" Paco saw she wore a marine outfit.

"I somewhat hit your car. I was—" Before she could even finish, Paco went outside.

"What the fuck, son!" Paco shouted, seeing his back tail light was mashed out by a GMC truck.

"I'm sorry, I was trying to park behind you and I went up too close," she cried. "You can take my name and insurance."

"No need for that. I'll buy a new car," Paco said, climbing in the driver's seat trying to conceal his anger.

"Look, I'm Mauda, is there any way I can still contact you?"

"For what? I told you it's okay, don't worry about it." Paco started up his car.

"I just wanna see you again, you're cute," she said, now catching his attention. The exchanged numbers before splitting ways.

***

Mott Haven Projects, BX
Two Weeks Later

Tonight was Halloween and everybody was out trick or treating, kids, teens, and adults. Paco was dressed up as Jason, walking through the projects to see kids and parents all dressed up in scary outfits for Halloween.

Paco made his way past a small crowd of thugs taking the stairs up to apartment 3B where he heard YG and PG had family at. Paco had an ex who lived in this same building, so she gave him a rundown on the brothers. Someone had to pay for Katty's death.

He knocked on the door.

"Trick or treat!" Paco shouted, holding a small bag with a gun inside. The door opened seconds later, and an older black woman with a son and bowl of candy approached.

"Ain't you a little too old to be—"

Boc, Boc, Boc, Boc, Boc...

Paco killed the woman and child. He looked at the door number again and realized it said 3D, not 3B. When he was going to 3B's door, the elevator door opened and YG and two goons stepped out and saw Mrs. Baldwin on the floor. They looked at the man with the Jason costume and gun, and started firing at him, knowing he was op.

Bloc, Bloc, Bloc, Bloc, Bloc, Bloc, Bloc, Bloc...

Boc, Boc, Boc—Click, click, click.

Paco's gun jammed, so he ran out the staircase knowing he had no wins. Paco ran out the basement level towards the back parking lot where Hasley was awaiting him.

Chapter 24

Walton Ave, Bronx

Less's mom, Brielle, was walking around with her old drug buddy, Rebel, who was a well-known heroin user. Brielle was clean for ten years until her son, Kip Loc, recently got murdered, then she relapsed and hit rock bottom. She lost her job, her apartment in Mill Brook, and herself.

They both walked into an abandoned building where they got high at and slept from time to time. Last night, Brielle and Rebel ran into Less in Lil' Italy, where they were coping drugs. When Less saw his mom, he literally chased her off the block in front of everybody. She was disappointed in herself for letting her son see her like this.

"Rebel, this my last night. I gotta get my life together." Brielle sat down on the boxes and coats they slept on.

"Oh, so you gonna just leave me out here alone again?" Rebel said, pulling out her needle and belt.

"You need to clean up too, Rebel. You got a family that loves you."

"Brielle, that's nice and all, but my life's been over since I contracted HIV," Rebel said, passing Brielle two needles, and one was hers.

"Have faith, God is good," Brielle said while getting the dope ready.

After remixing the dope, Brielle poured it into her needle and tied a belt around her good arm where she still had a few good veins. When she shot it in her arm, it hit her head but the feeling was different.

Brielle felt her body overheat and her heart started to race. Her body went into extreme shock, leaving foam pouring out her nose and mouth.

Rebel stood up, not knowing if she was dead or not, and ran for her life. She didn't want to be part of no murder scene.

***

Webster Pjs, Bx
Next Day

Less was drinking a bottle of Henny, trying to hold back his tears as he thought about the loss of his mother. When he got the news of Brielle's body being found, he was sick. The other day, when he caught his mom coming out of a drug spot, he wanted to kill her.

His mother was doing so well for herself before she went backwards. He went to the hospital this morning, and they informed him she died from some type of acid in her veins. Less's homies all reached out to him on social media when he posted up an old pic of his mom and brothers. He had received over 20,800 likes in a matter of 24 hours.

There had to be some type of foul play in his mom's death, because one thing he knew for sure was, his mom ain't fuck with no acid, only crack and dope.

While he was sitting there mourning listening to some old DMX, it hit him. Less saw Rebel with his mother the other day, and she was bad news. Rebel was one of the feins everybody knew. She used to be a big drug dealer's wife before he got killed.

Less grabbed his hoodie and Glock 40, rushing out his crib. He knew something was off, and he was going to find out.

***

Fulton Ave, BX

Rebel had just snuck into Katcha Park late at night with a young hustler named Mel B. All the young hustlers loved Rebel because she looked decent for a fein. She was thick, high yellow, and had perky tits and a crazy head game.

Her pussy was trash, but she would only let niggas fuck if they wore condoms. She didn't let nobody fuck her raw because she wasn't trying to go back to jail for attempted murder.

When they got to the table, she pulled down her dirty jeans and bent over, showing her wide ass and hairy bush. Mel B put a condom on and slid in her, grabbing her waist.

"Oh, shit, fuck that pussy!" she shouted.

Mel B pumped in and out of her, spitting on his dick to get her moist. Rebel made all types of fake sex noises while he pounded her back out.

"Ohhhhh, Mel, yesssss, babyyy..."

He picked up the pace, unable to cum, so he pulled out and took the condom off. Her pussy was trash. Rebel felt him pull out and knew he wanted some head, so she got on her knees. Rebel wrapped her large lips around the mushroom area, sucking fast and slow.

"Uhmmmmmmm, fuck," Mel B said, closing eyes picturing Beyoncé was sucking him off.

When she went deep onto his shaft, she heard a loud ... *Pop!* She felt his body collapse on her, making her roll over.

"You think you slick, bitch?" Less stated, forcing his gun in her mouth. "Why you poison my mom, bitch? You got one chance," he stated, now placing his gun to her head.

"Glock paid me 1,000 dollars to do it. Please, I didn't want to do it, but I had no choice. He said he would kill my son." Rebel was in tears.

"I hope it was worth it," Less said before he blew her brains out, leaving the park, stepping over Mel B's dead body.

Romell Tukes

Chapter 25

Pelham, BX

Capri was inside of her beautiful suburban home watching an HBO six-part true crime documentary series about a serial killer. Laying on her stomach in her boy shorts showing her thick thighs and curves, Capri was a sight to see.

She was Native American, raised on a reservation in upstate New York. When she moved to the Bronx, she met a man by the name of Austin and fell in love. At the time, Capri was unaware her boyfriend was a drug dealer, and a kingpin at that. He ended up getting arrested and leaving her tons of bricks to continue where he left off.

With her boyfriend serving a life sentence, she took over and found a new plug named Fats who was about his business, just like her. Capri sold drugs in Westchester County and the Newbury area. She was queen pin status. She lived alone, but she had condos in Brooklyn, Yonkers, Miami, and Atlanta.

Her show was just about over, but Capri was so tired, she paused it and walked into her master bathroom to take a shower so she could get ready for bed. After taking an hour shower, the bathroom was steamy and foggy. Capri walked back into her room ass naked to see two men standing there with guns, looking at her nice body.

"What a surprise," she said, walking right past Black and Paco to grab her robe off her hook on the closet door.

Black looked at how phat her ass was and felt himself get an erection.

"Bro, get yourself together." Paco saw how lost Black was in her physical appearance, but Paco couldn't deny how good she looked.

"I guess it's been you two parked down the block for two days watching my house? Better than the feds. Let me take a guess, you want money and drugs? I heard about your little crew." Capri sat down on the edge of her bed tying her robe, giving them a last look at her nice shaved peach fuzz.

"Since you know what we want, where is it?" Paco stated, not falling for her games. He'd met many women like her.

"There are two bags in the garage under the red Rolls Royce Wraith," she stated, playing with her long nails.

Paco looked at Black who was staring at Capri, trying to look up her thick legs to see her kitty cat again.

"Nigga, go to the garage, creep ass nigga." Paco pushed Black out his zone.

"Aight, son, and don't push me again. I'll shoot your soft ass," Black said, walking off seeing Capri laugh.

"What's your name? That's the least I can know before you rob, rape, or kill me," Capri asked, looking into his eyes, which turned her on.

"Satan."

"Funny, ummmm... If I live, I won't have you killed if you let me get some of that," she stated, looking at his hard manhood poking out his pants.

Paco was embarrassed. There was nothing he could do or say. Capri was a bad bitch, she would turn any man on.

"You think I'll fuck you so you can kill me? Who the fuck do I look like, a mental patient?" Paco looked at her.

"I'm just saying, you don't have to rob me. I can put you and your crew onto some real money. Y'all will never have to rob again," Capri replied.

"There are only two problems with that, ma. One is you work for the enemy—"

"I work for myself. I buy work from Fats, but I can find a new plug any day," she shot back, offended.

"For two, we jack boyz, ma, we not so much into selling drugs. We be giving that shit away," Paco said, seeing Black come back in the room smiling.

"That's a lot of shit. We good to leave, bro. Did she ask about me?" Black said seriously.

"I'll meet you outside," Paco told him.

110

"You always get to have the fun," Black replied.

"Bye, chocolate," Capri said, seeing him leave.

"Your seduction game is good, but not good enough for a playa who mastered it," Paco told her before shooting her six times in her upper torso.

Paco saw her eyelids close and made his way outside, thinking if Capri could have been beneficial alive, besides being a good fuck.

***

Burnside, Bronx

YG and PG's mom, Carrie, was leaving Morris Heights Medical Center at 10:35 pm. Today was a long day at work, but she was glad it was over. Her feet were killing her. She called PG on FaceTime.

Carrie climbed in her car, but before she could close her door, someone snatched it open and attacked her with a knife. The attacker covered Carrie's mouth with his hand while he rammed the long kitchen knife in and out of her.

After stabbing her twenty-four times, she was dead and lifeless. Less saw her phone was on her lap and someone was on FaceTime. When he saw it was PG, he smiled.

"What's poppin', bro," Less said into the phone, seeing PG cry.

"I'ma kill you, nigga!" PG screamed into the phone before Less disconnected the FaceTime call.

Less speed walked across the lot where Black was waiting on him.

"You took forever, son," Black said, seeing blood all over Less's hands as he climbed in the truck.

"Nigga, shut up and drive. You been getting on my nerves all day," Less said, using wet wipes to clean the blood stains off his hands.

"Kazzy and Paco just called. They want us to come to Club Angle in Queens," Black said, hopping on the highway.

***

Queens, NY
An Hour Later

The strip club was litty tonight. Kazzy, Black, Less, and Paco had a VIP section full of dancers and bottles, having the time of their lives.

The split from the Capri robbery had the men back on top. Kazzy had the whole Mill Brook area on lock with drugs. He flooded the streets and he planned to continue to flood the hood, but he needed a solid plug.

Kazzy talked to the men about finding a plug and everybody agreed, but nobody planned to give up jacking drug dealers. This was a new chapter for the crew. Kazzy was gonna tell Knight in the morning that they were opening shop.

Chapter 26

Norfolk, VA

"You see all them niggas posted up on the pjs?" Uncle Slim told Knight while he drove slow through the hood.

Knight saw a gang of young hoodlums standing around in black t-shirts, looking around for feins and the police, who they called rollers.

"Yeah, what's up with them?" Knight asked, seeing four crackheads walking up the block.

"They work for me, this my hood. Who you know come fresh home to his own turf?" Uncle Slim parked in front of an apartment building connected to ten others.

Since Knight had been in VA, he saw everybody treat his uncle with the utmost respect, as if he was a legend here. Last night in the club, everybody showed Uncle Slim love. Hustlers, killers, pimps, and hoes all went out their way to greet him.

"You doing your thing out here, Unc," Knight said while they walked into a small apartment where seven females were at tables cutting dope and bagging it up.

Knight saw so many keys all over the crib, he thought he was in a locksmith store.

"Damn," was all Knight could say.

"This is why I called you down here. I want you to join me, nephew. That jacking shit is played out and it's the fastest way to a casket. Karma is a bitch. You will become a millionaire in a matter of months. How many niggas you got to rob to see 100 racks? I need a real solid gangsta like you, because these country niggas play dirty and they untrustworthy," Uncle Slim stated, walking into the kitchen where two men were cooking piles of coke.

"What you had in mind?" Knight asked.

"I got a hood across town I want you to run, it's all you. I'll be supplying the keyz, I just need you to run the hood and control shit. If you gotta bust your gun, bust it. If you have to smoke a nigga, smoke him. But this ain't the Bronx, nephew, we on big money status now," Uncle Slim said, walking out the trap.

"What's the price on them birds?"

"For you, twenty."

"Twenty? It must be stepped on twenty times if you giving them to me for that price. Something ain't right," Knight stated.

"Nah, I just got an amazing plug. He's like a brother to me. We're about to go meet him now, but before we do, what you gonna do?" Uncle Slim asked, stopping near his driver's side door.

"I'm down, under one condition."

"And what's that?" Uncle Slim was praying it wasn't no crazy, off-the-wall shit, because he knew how his nephew got down. He heard stories while in the feds about him and D Fatal Brim.

"Let me run shit how I want to and stay out my way," Knight requested.

"Ok, we got a deal, nephew. Let's go meet Gotti. He can't wait to see ya." Uncle Slim got in the car, happy as he could be.

***

Manhattan, NY

Bankroll and a large number of men and women from Soundview were on a party bus having a good time, smoking and drinking. The party bus was taking the crew to the second club of the night near Webster Hall.

Bankroll was out to celebrate his sister's birthday. He hadn't been outta Soundview in months, too focused on getting money and taking care of his new seed. He was still hunting down Knight's crew. Word was they had Mill Brook pjs and Webster pjs on lock, checking a big bag.

Glock was ducked off on the Lower Eastside while he made YG and PG do his foot work. Bankroll ain't respect that at all, but he knew Glock wasn't an official killer like Dollar, Glock's brother who was in the army.

Bankroll lost so many good homies in the past couple of months. He wanted to get out the game, but he knew he couldn't shit on Glock.

"Thanks for coming out, brother!" his sister Erin shouted, drunk, leaning all over him.

"Ok, Erin, get your ass off me." Bankroll pushed her off him.

"My homegirl over there said what's up, she trying to see what that piece hitting on." Erin laughed and called her girl over.

Bankroll and his sister's friend talked, and she was trying fuck right on the bus, but he told her after the club they could get low at a hotel. He saw how thick she was and he knew he was going to have a blast with her thick ass.

At the club, everybody got out except a few, who were knocked out on the couch. When Bankroll stepped off the bus, his sister was two inches in front of him.

Two men ran from the shadows across the street and started letting off shots back to back. Bankroll pushed Erin to the floor, shooting back at the shooters. The shooters hit the thick chick he made plans with later, in her head.

Boc, Boc, Boc, Boc, Boc, Boc, Boc, Boc, Boc...

Bloc, Bloc, Bloc, Bloc, Bloc...

People were getting hit trying to run back into the bus, while Bankroll hit one of the men, making him drop his weapon. When Bankroll saw Erin was safe on the bus, he got inside and the driver pulled off, speeding down the thin one-way street.

Bankroll saw Paco and Kazzy's faces. He knew he was being followed now. Six people from the party bus were left dead in front of the club.

Romell Tukes

Chapter 27

Highbridge, Bronx

Detective Woodberry was driving through the Highbridge area on her way to visit a woman who was a witness to a double murder two nights ago in the Highbridge projects.

She'd been so busy at work getting hammered with caseload after caseload, she forgot what regular life was like. Her relationship with Fats was getting stronger by the day, and things were starting to get a little more serious.

Woodberry parked in front of the building and saw the woman she was coming to see walking up the block.

"Mrs., are you Dennis?" Woodberry asked.

"Yes." Dennis looked across the street to see a group of thugs watching her talk to the police, which was a death wish in the hood.

"You want to go somewhere and talk about the murders you saw?" Detective Woodberry saw all the hoodlums across the street staring at her and Dennis.

Detective Woodberry took on the case because a ten-year-old black girl was killed on her way home from a youth center by a stray bullet. The Highbridge niggas were beefing with another hood in the South Bronx, and the killing was going back and forth.

"I'm sorry, Ms., but I don't know what you're talking about," the woman said, rushing off inside her apartment building.

Detective Woodberry knew she was scared, but that was only because of the drug dealers across the street smirking. She walked across the street toward the group of youngsters on the corner in front of the store.

"Y'all think killing a little girl who was innocent makes y'all tough or gangsta!" she shouted so they could all hear her.

One of the young men stood up from the milk crate.

"That was my niece, so before you come over here running your mouth, get your facts straight," the man stated.

"So, you're the cause of your niece's death. That makes you feel like a real man?" she replied, seeing him get upset while everybody stood in silence because he ran the block.

"You don't know shit about these streets. You run around in your Uncle Tom suit forgettin' where you came from and who you are, while we stuck in the struggle. People die every day, son. Like it or not, we can never bring a life back, but it's blood for blood in these streets. So, if you ain't making no arrest, I suggest you get off the block before where you standing at becomes a candlelight service," the man said seriously.

In the last month, three cops were killed in this neighborhood. Police didn't even drive through the area anymore unless it was a crime scene.

Detective Woodberry felt her phone ring and turned to walk off, not trying to argue or get killed. It was Fats calling her, asking where she was at. She told him in Highbridge, and he told her to meet him at the middle school on Ogden Ave, and she agreed.

***

Detective Woodberry parked next to Fats' big boy truck with tints. Fats hopped out in a clean suit with some roses and a box of chocolate.

"Hey, babe," she told Fats when he climbed in her car, kissing her lips.

"What's up, sexy, these are for you." He handed her the items, seeing her perfect smile.

"Thank you."

"How's work? I just wanted to see you before I go out of town," Fats stated.

"Work is good, but where you going? I had plans for us tonight. I'm horny and off my period, so you know I need that D," she said, laughing.

"I don't think you'll be getting no more D for a long time," Fats said in an evil tone as she caught on.

"What?" she replied, seeing him reach for something.

BOOM, BOOM, BOOM, BOOM...

Her brains stained the car windows. Fats cleaned the gun and placed it in her hand to make it look like a suicide. He left her body there, hopping in his truck with Glock. When Glock recently told Fats who Black's mom was, he was fucked up it was Woodberry, because he was really starting to grow real feelings for her.

Fats knew what he had to do, because if Black would have found out Fats was fucking his mom, then he would've been a dead man.

One thing Fats had to admit was he respected Knight, Kazzy, Paco, Less, and Black's gangsta. They were a different type of young niggas. He wished he had them on his team instead of Glock, who was scared to death, and Fats saw it. He lost a lot of respect for him.

***

Yonkers, NY

Getty Square was a small shopping area on a four-way street in Yonkers. Less and Kazzy walked into the Cell Phone Repair store and put the *we're closed* sign on the door.

When the two workers saw this, they reached for their weapons, already knowing what time it was!

PSST, PSST, PSST, PSST, PSST...

Less shot one of the men all in his upper chest, dropping him, making the other man think twice about pulling out his weapon.

"Take it easy," the man stated with his hands in the air.

"You work for Glock, and I know he hid a stash in here because I saw him come in here twice in one week, bro," Kazzy stated, pointing the silencer on his Glock 40 at his head.

"It's a bag in the back inside the small locker in the bottom. That's what he left for us to sell, man. I don't even fuck with that nigga, I just met him through Olivia, his baby mother," the man cried as Less went to get the bag.

"His baby mother?"

"Yeah, she lives on White Plains Road in Gun Hill Projects. He got two baby mothers, I think."

"Aight..."

PSST, PSST...

Kazzy fired twice while Less came out with a bag of coke bricks in a duffle bag. Even though they had drugs moving in the Bronx, they refused to give up robbing niggas, especially Glock's people. It was free bandz.

Chapter 28

Richmond, VA
Two Months Later

Gotti and Uncle Slim were riding in the back of Gotti's Maybach, on the way to a big mansion party.

"How's your nephew doing?" Gotti asked, smoking a cigar, trying not to get ashes on his Armani suit.

"He's doing good already. He's moving 30 keys a week, better than the other crews," Slim added, proud of Knight taking over Norfolk slowly but surely.

"Good, I like him, he seems loyal. I want him around," Gotti stated.

Gotti was the biggest drug lord in VA, and he controlled a lot of the drug trade in other states.

"I see a bright future for him." Uncle Slim knew Knight had always been a born hustler, just like Knight's father was.

"I'm glad you're home and have that time back. I missed you. Besides my real brothers, I consider you family to me more than anybody," said Gotti.

"It's the same here, Gotti. You know how I do, I'ma real nigga. You blessed me and I returned it with loyalty."

"True, one thing I realized in life is when a person does good, then it always comes back, and the same goes for when a person does bad."

"That's a fact." Uncle Slim saw the car pulling up to a large gate surrounding one of the biggest mansions he'd ever seen.

There was a big party being thrown by an NBA player Gotti knew for some time now, so he wasn't missing this party for nothing.

***

Bankroll's older brother, Tee, just came home from doing ten years in the feds for guns and drugs. Tee was at a halfway house on Fordham Road, which was filled with other federal prisoners just coming home. It was 7 am and Tee had to go job hunting, because his probation officer was on his body about finding a job or he was going back to prison.

Tee didn't fuck with his brother, Bankroll, because while he was locked up, his brother did nothing for him, and Bankroll got his girlfriend pregnant. Fresh home out of prison with no money or support was the worst feeling. He was still wearing the gray sweatshirt he left prison in last week.

Before going job hunting, Tee walked across the street to the park to feed the birds as he did every morning. When he went to sit down, he saw a man in a black Champion hoodie approach him. It was cold out this morning, and snowy, but winter was almost over.

"What's up, son," the man said, sitting down on the bench next to Tee.

"What's good, black man," Tee replied, looking at the trees thinking about his future.

"I'm sure you'll be at a better place soon."

"I hope so," Tee replied before the man shot him three times in his head.

Black got up and ran off through the park. Black was on a killing spree since the death of his mother. The news labeled it a suicide, but Black knew it was Glock or his people. Black knew his mom better than anybody, and she wasn't the type to harm anyone or herself.

***

Pelham, Bronx

Less got up with one of his exes he saw last week in City Island. She was looking like a snack. He knocked on her front door with a bottle of Henny in his hands. Paradise opened the door wearing a silk robe with nothing under, showing her big nipples on her DD breasts.

"Hey, Less, come in," Paradise stated, walking off making her ass sway a little extra than her normal walk.

Less's dick got hard. He knew it was going to be a long night, so he needed the Henny to give him that extra strength.

"You want some Henny, ma?" Less said, walking through her nice clean house.

"Nah, I got some wine upstairs, come on," she said, taking him upstairs, giving him a full view of what he ain't have in years.

Once in the room, she drank some wine and sat on his lap, feeling his hard-on.

"I missed you, Less," she whispered into his ear, licking it.

"Show me," he replied, taking a sip of liquor.

Paradise smiled and got on the floor. She undid his belt buckle and placed his rod in her warm, wet mouth. She made love to his mic, spitting on it then going deep until he hit the back of her throat.

Less tried to enjoy the show, but something in the closet caught his attention when the door moved. Not one to wait to be killed, he grabbed his gun and fired into the closet nine times. He kicked Paradise on the floor and went to open the closet door to see two men with guns both shot up. One was still breathing before he put one in his head.

Paradise tried to run until he shot her in the ass cheek. "Ahhhhhhh!" she screamed.

"Who sent your dumb ass to do this?"

"Bankroll. I swear, I ain't—"

Boc, Boc...

Less shot her in her long neck before fixing his clothes and leaving, mad she fucked his nut up.

Romell Tukes

Chapter 29

Manhattan, NY
Two Months Later

Oliva and Kazzy were on their fourth date. The two had been attached to each other since they were in Times Square for New Year's Eve when the ball dropped. They hadn't made things official as of yet, but it was getting to that point. They had sex daily, and it was the best they both ever had.

Tonight, they were at the Peter Luger Steakhouse on the outside balcony enjoying their meal.

"I'm glad you could make time for me today, Chris," Olivia stated while staring at him.

"Anytime, I know I've been busy, but I'm focused on us and building something real, because nowadays, it's hard to find good, beautiful women." Kazzy was looking at Olivia's breasts while he talked, because she was the perfect woman. The only bad thing was, she was Glock's baby mother.

Oliva never talked about Glock because there was nothing for her to talk about. She disliked him and he was a deadbeat father.

Kazzy never told her who he really was, except his name was Chris and he was getting money. He tried to keep his distance so she didn't find out who he really was. At first, he was just fucking with Olivia to get close to Glock, but he started falling deep for her.

"Can I ask you something?" she asked.

"Anything, ma."

"You really care for me?" Olivia asked seriously.

"Yeah, and I love getting to know you," he replied.

"So, you would never lie to me?"

"I wouldn't lie to you, but I may hold some things back to prevent from hurting you."

"What's the difference? Why not keep it real with me?" She was getting frustrated.

Kazzy wondered where all of this was coming from, because Olivia was the type of woman who didn't ask too many questions.

"Where are you going with this?"

"You're not who I thought you were, Kazzy Loc from Mill Brook projects who wants to kill my baby father," Olivia started then took a sip of wine.

Kazzy was at a loss for words. He ain't know whether to get up and leave or lie to her.

"It's okay, I hate that bitch nigga. All you had to do was ask, and I would have told you everything about that deadbeat," she said. "But you ain't have to use me." She sounded hurt.

"I didn't use you, Olivia. I'm really feeling you." Kazzy felt like shit.

"Shhhh...just stop, please. I just want to know if you was gonna kill me like how you do everybody else," she asked.

"No, if I was gonna kill you, I would have been did it in Times Square," Kazzy replied, and for some reason, she believed him.

"What do you want to know?"

"Everything." Kazzy liked her so much more now for being honest.

They talked about Glock for an hour, and she gave Kazzy everything he needed to know. Her only problem was her son growing up without a father, but he was already fatherless.

Kazzy and Olivia went back to her crib in Gun Hill and made love all night. They even confessed their love for each other.

***

Albany, NY

Paco and Mauda were both driving on the highway to the suburbs located outside of upstate New York City, called Albany. Mauda was raised in Albany with her two brothers, mother, and father.

She and Paco had been together since the first time they chilled together. She was into him deeply, so deeply she had threesomes with him and Hasley almost every night.

Mauda was AWOL from the army, so she was wanted. She didn't want to go back. She wanted to be with Paco so bad, Mauda became a stick-up girl with him.

Tonight, they were driving to Mauda's brother's house, who was a kingpin. Paco was the only person who Mauda told she used to get raped by her older brother when she was a little girl.

"You good, ma?" Paco asked, holding her hand, seeing she was lost into the night stars as Paco did 80 mph down the highway coming to their exit.

"I'm good, daddy, just thinking I'm glad I met you, papi. Since I've met you, I feel like I found my true self, because all the army did for me was brainwash me," she spoke honestly.

In the army, soldiers would rape women, mentally abuse them, and discourage them from being who they really were. Mauda remained strong minded and solid while in training and overseas, but she was trying her best to be someone else.

"I got you now," Paco stated, listening to the GPS monitor take them in a nice area.

"I hope so," she said calmly.

***

Dewatoy was at home enjoying dinner with his family, his wife and daughter, who was a freshman in high school. He had a beautiful family whom he loved to death. His wife was the city hall clerk, and he was the biggest dope boy in Albany. He supplied the whole city from uptown to downtown.

"How was your day, baby?" Dewatoy asked his beautiful daughter as they enjoyed the meal his wife prepared.

"It was good, Dad. I passed two tests, so I'm a little happy about that," his daughter replied, seeing her aunty and a Spanish kid walk in with big assault rifles.

When Dewatoy saw his sister, he almost choked because he knew karma would one day come back around from when he used to rape her.

"I'm all grown up now, Dewatoy. I won't let you rape me now."
Boc...
Mauda shot her brother in his arm.

His wife looked like she was about to run to the phone as she got up. Paco shot her twice in the chest and he shot his daughter in the head. Dewatoy had tears in his eyes. He couldn't believe what was happening.

"Where is the shit, Dewatoy?"

"In the garage, in the ceiling," Dewatoy said as Paco asked her was she good, because he was running off to get the money.

Dewatoy started begging for his life in Spanish, but Mauda laughed at him before shooting him six times in his face.

There was so much money and drugs in the ceiling, Paco and Mauda made two trips back and forth, loading up the truck.

Chapter 30

Rikers Island Jail, Queens

YG was in jail for a bullshit DWI and a hit-and-run charge from two nights ago when he left a strip club drunk. He was glad they ain't find his gun in the stash spot of the car, or he would have been sick, because New York state was giving three and a half years for a gun charge, first offense.

Walking to his unit in the five building, he saw a bunch of Bloods throwing up gang signs to see if he was banging. YG was down with a crew called Young Gunnerz. They were deep in certain hoods of the Bronx, but they also had a lot of beef with other gangs.

There were two young niggas standing on the tier when he entered five, one of the worst units in the building. This wasn't YG's first time in the Rock, as most called it, so he knew what was up and what he had to do to stay alive.

Razor tag was heavy in the jail. It was when prisoners would cut each other's faces with razors or any sharp object to leave a long scar on a nigga's face they called buck fifties.

"Yo, son, where you from?" a big young nigga asked, flexing his big muscles wearing a gold rope chain.

"I'm from BX, what's good." YG put his bags and bed roll down just in case he had to get it poppin'. He was all for it.

"You bangin', skrap?" another prisoner asked, checking out his tattoos.

"Nah, I'm gunning. I'm YG."

"Oh, iight, bro, we fuck with y'all in this unit. We all Blood Hounds, bro. It's seven Young Gunners on the tier, pull up. I'm Lil' Blazer, and this big guy is Hef from Brooklyn," Lil' Blazer said, shifting YG to the unit.

The first night went well. YG knew almost half the block and word got around that he was a real live killer, so he was good. He and Lil' Blazer got real close. They knew a lot of the same people, even though Lil' Blazer was from Soundview projects.

***

Cortland Projects, BX

PG just left out the back of building 87 where his motorcycle was parked. It was early in the morning and a little chilly outside, so he wore a ski mask and a hoodie.

Last night, PG was at his side bitch's crib drinking and fucking all night. He'd been laying low since his mom died, trying to wait on the perfect time to kill his ops. Word was, Kazzy Loc and his crew were now getting big time money all over the Bronx, so PG knew they were also getting their numbers up by making allies with other hoods.

When PG hopped on his bike, he saw two undercover cop cars speed towards him. PG pulled out his weapon doing the first thing that came to mind.

Boc, Boc, Boc, Boc, Boc, Boc, Boc...

He killed a cop in the passenger seat of one of the cars.

PG raced off out the lot, hitting 90 mph down the street swerving through lanes and busses. It didn't take long for him to lose the cops, but now he had bigger problems on his plate than what the police were coming to get him for.

PG called Glock so he could find somewhere to get low, because the Bronx wasn't the best place for him being wanted for killing a cop.

***

Norfolk, VA

Knight was making a lot of money in VA, he even bought a little house on the outskirts of Norfolk. His uncle was doing the right thing. He never knew there was so much money outside of the Bronx.

Kazzy called him every day to inform him on what was going on. He heard Paco just hit a big lick, so they were doing good with no plug.

Knight wanted to supply his brother with work, but he needed that jump start. Last week, one of Knight's workers was telling him about some kingpin nigga that went by the name CL. So he was on the end of the block, waiting for CL to come to his side bitch's crib.

CL's side bitch's brother told Knight that CL was hiding work in his sister's closet, but he was too scared to rob him because CL was connected.

A Bentley coupe pulled into the small driveway, making Knight smile as he put on his ski mask and grabbed his Glock 45 with a 30-round clip. Knight jumped out, creeping up the block, seeing CL going inside of his trunk.

"Stand up," Knight said, pointing his gun to the back of CL's head as he followed orders.

"It's all in the trunk, bruh."

"Nigga, shut up, go inside the house, and any false moves, you dead," Knight said while CL walked up the stairs inside his house.

When the door opened, CL's side chick ran to jump in her baby's arms, and met a gunshot wound to the head.

"Damn, dawg, she ain't do shit, bruh," CL cried out because she was two months pregnant with his seed.

"Go to the bedroom where your shit at, or you next." Knight followed him to the back of the house.

Once in the room, CL grabbed two blue laundry bags full of drugs and passed them to him.

"That's it," CL said, hearing his iPhone go off. Knight took his phone out his hand to see the name was under Brother, and the picture was of Gotti, who Knight met a few times.

Knight knew he'd fucked up, but he knew it was too late to turn back now.

"Get down on the floor," Knight told him as he grabbed a long rope he saw hanging in the closet and hog tied CL.

Knight carried the two bags outside and grabbed the money out the trunk of the Bentley.

131

He hoped leaving him alive wouldn't backfire, but he knew shit would get ugly if he killed CL, who he assumed was Gotti's brother.

Chapter 31

Dear, Delaware

Paco was driving on a long, narrow interstate where the speed limit was under 35 mph. State troopers were parked in the cuts near almost every exit, thirsty to pull someone over.

He was on his way to rob a big-time drug dealer named Kenny, who had most of Delaware on lock. Paco heard about him through one of his clients he was selling grams to. His boy told him Kenny was taxing niggas on the work in Delaware, but niggas had nowhere else to go.

Delaware niggas were scared to go to Philly or New Jersey to get drugs, because they didn't want to risk going to jail. When Paco got the scoop on Kenny, he came up with a plan he was going to put into motion today.

Paco got off exit 37 driving through some trailer park, which was known as a high drug area. He and his crew had been getting money in the Bronx day and night all over, but old habits were hard to break. The crew was still robbing shit left and right.

He pulled up next to a big mobile home with two luxury cars parked in the front.

***

Inside the trailer mobile home, Kenny had the beautiful Spanish woman he met two nights ago at a local bar bent over on the edge of his bed.

"Ahhhahhh, fuck!" she screamed while Kenny spread her ass cheeks, going deep into her walls.

Her shit was so good, Kenny wanted to dance as he fucked her hard and rough from behind.

Kenny was a twenty-five-year-old kingpin who sold keys of coke for double what he was buying them for. He had a Philly plug who was tossing him keys on the arm just because he was going to bring the money back.

133

Kenny felt his nut building up, then he felt something slam against the side of his head, knocking him to the floor.

"What the fuck..." Kenny was ass naked on the floor, looking at Paco with a gun in his hand. Kenny knew everybody from the Dear area, but Paco didn't look familiar.

The Spanish woman got dressed in her skirt and blouse then kissed Paco on his cheek because she was sucking dick earlier.

"Good job, baby, go outside and warm the car up while I take care of this clown," Paco told her, slapping her ass.

"Ok, papi, bye Kenny," Hasley said, walking out.

"She had some good pussy, trust me, I know, but let's make this easy. I'm pressed for time," Paco told him, checking his AP watch.

"I got 30 bricks of fishkill and a bag of money with 300,000 in the grill out back, it's all yours. I just want—" Kenny's words were cut off by bullets.

Once he was dead, Paco went outside to the back to see three gym bags filled with drugs and money. He grabbed everything then Hasley drove back to the Bronx while Paco took a nap.

***

Manhattan Federal Court, NY
Two Months Later

Today was D Fatal Brim's big day. He was in his fourth and last day of trial. He was nervous as he sat in front of the white older female judge who'd been giving him dirty looks all day because he was being accused of murdering an innocent woman.

Eight of the jurors were females, which was a bad look for him, but he trusted his lawyer who had a lot of good arguments. One of his main arguments was, on the FaceTime video, they couldn't really see his face, so it could have been anybody who killed Yasmin, Glock's baby mother.

"We'll be ok, Bud," D Fatal Brim's lawyer stated with confidence.

The juror handed the judge a piece of paper with his destiny on it.

"It seems as if a decision has been made," the judge stated, putting on her glasses to see clearly.

"By the state of New York in the Second Circuit District of the Supreme Court, I hereby declare that Mr. Harrison is guilty of all counts including the murder of Yasmin Galilei!" the judge shouted through the court.

D Fatal Brim's face was in shock as he wanted to cry, but tears wouldn't form.

"I sentence you to life in federal prison. I hope you use this time well, Mr. Harrison. Have a good day," she stated before hitting her gavel then leaving.

D Fatal Brim left the courtroom feeling like his life was just stolen from him in a matter of minutes.

***

Soundview, Bronx

Bankroll walked past two of his workers as he went into the corner store to buy a single Newport. The past couple of months, Bankroll had been outta town opening up shop in different cities. He had a crew of his boys getting money in his hood, but he was selling keys almost double for what he was getting them for.

Since the murder of Bankroll's brother, he'd been sending hits to any niggas who were down with Kazzy and his crew. In the past five days, a total of eleven people had been killed due to the Soundview and MillBrook projects beef.

Bodies were dropping all over the city, so both sides were on point for the most part. Bankroll was playing the hood hard, letting niggas know he ran shit and they weren't backing down.

An all-black Nissan Maxima busted a U-turn across the street while Bankroll came out of the store. Bankroll saw the whole play and went for his gun at the same time he saw a nigga climb out the Wingfield with a Draco.

Tat, tat, tat, tat, tat, tat...
Bloc, Bloc, Bloc...

135

Tat-tat-tat-tat...

One of Bankroll's workers, Millz, caught four to the chest. The car raced off down the block. Bankroll and his other soldier left Millz to die on the same corner his brother died two weeks ago.

Chapter 32

Mott Haven Projects, BX

PG was in his crib on his back while a woman's face was buried in his pole, pleasing him with her mouth.

"Shhhh..." PG moaned, feeling the back of her throat while she gripped his balls.

She swallowed his whole pipe with her nonexistent gag reflex. His shaft slid in and out her mouth as her jaws clenched tight, sucking him in.

PG came hard, so hard he closed his eyes until she sucked his cum out of him. When he was done, the female got up and went to spit it out and rinse her mouth out with mouthwash. PG looked at her curves and phat ass and got horny again.

He met her a couple of days ago at a Dyckman basketball game, and he'd been on her ever since. She showed up at his crib wearing a peacoat with nothing under it. This was only round one, and he couldn't wait for her to come out the bathroom for round two.

"I'm trying to see what that pussy like, babe!" PG yelled, on the bed playing with his meat.

"I don't think that's going to happen tonight," Mauda said, walking out the bathroom with a gun pointed at him.

PG's gun was all the way across the room on the dresser, so he knew getting to it was over.

"Let's talk about this, ma. I will pay you double whatever," PG stated, watching her every move.

"PG, it's no price on love, and your fucking dick stank." She'd been wanting to tell him that all night.

"Bitch, fuck you."

"I'll pass on that. You gotta step your game up first," Mauda said while looking at his shrimp.

Bloc, Bloc, Bloc, Bloc, Bloc...

PG's body was riddled with bullets from a 44 Mag Bulldog.

When his body wasn't moving anymore, Mauda grabbed her peacoat and walked out the building where Paco was awaiting her in the back lot.

***

Norfolk, VA

Knight met a bad redbone chick two weeks ago in a club in Richmond. They kicked it off good, and their vibes were strong over the phone and in person.

This was the first chick he met and was really feeling since he'd been in VA. He liked her attitude and swag. Stephen had her own bag, which he liked about her. Plus, she was different.

Today, he was about to go on a yacht with her. It was her date, so Knight played along, hoping to get in her panties, but he could tell she wasn't that type of woman.

He pulled up to a small boat dock full of boats and yachts lined up. Looking around, he saw Stephen in a two-piece bikini waving him down from the biggest yacht.

"Damn," Knight said to himself, seeing her thick thighs covered in tatts.

Once on the boat, Stephen hugged him tightly.

"You look nice in your little Dior outfit," she said, looking him up and down with her colorful eyes.

"Thanks, this shit is fly."

"It's ok, but I plan to buy a new one in a couple of months," she stated, walking to the upper deck where she had a table full of fruits.

"All this for us?" he said, seeing the nice setup on the table.

"Yesss, as you know I'm vegan, so all I eat is this." She got a plate and passed him one.

"When this thang gonna sail out?" Knight asked, seeing her sit down.

"The captain's pulling off now. Let me find out you scared of the ocean," she said.

"Only if you knew. I'm from the Bronx, we don't swim or play in pods, ma."

"So I hear, but what brings you down to VA?" she asked.

"I just needed a getaway."

"Just like every other New York nigga that comes down here," she replied smiling, eating cherries.

"Let's just say, the same reason why you out here is the reason why I'm in D.C." She gave him a small wink.

"Understood." Knight was attracted to her beauty. He couldn't stop staring at her.

"The main reason why I called you out on this beautiful evening is because I know who you are, Knight," she said.

"Who am I?"

"You robbed CL, and sooner or later, Gotti will find out and have you killed," she said.

Knight gave her a look like he was ready to kill her.

"Who sent you and what the fuck you want?"

"I don't want nothing except you, and you know who I am, but what I know is a different matter. I'm Gotti's little sister and I'm his competition. I took over D.C. and I let him have VA after he snaked me out a Colombian plug, but luckily, I found a new plug," she admitted.

"Wow, so you knew who I was when you met me."

"Factz, I couldn't help but peep you that night, you had a mouth full of diamonds," she said laughing.

"So where does this lead us?"

"Into a bright future," she stated, rubbing his face, leaning in to kiss him. One thing led to another, and they were fucking all over the boat.

Chapter 33

Williamsburg, BX

Olivia had her son with her, getting him dressed so he could go out with his father to a Yankee game. This was the second time Glock called to spend time with his son since he was born. Glock was a deadbeat father, and she was ok with that. She had no issue raising a child alone.

"Mommy, I have to take a piss," her son said while she was tying his sneaker.

"Ok, baby, hurry up." Olivia heard her doorbell ring.

She and Kazzy were in a real relationship, and she was starting to fall in love with him. She knew his lifestyle, but that was always the type of man she went for.

Olivia had been bringing Kazzy around her son and family. She felt comfortable with him and she had a feeling he would turn out to be the one.

Opening the door, she saw Glock standing on the other side.

"Can I come in?" he said with a serious look on his face.

"Why not." Oliva moved over, letting him inside.

"Nice place, I ain't know welfare give out shit like this," Glock said, being funny.

"Ask your mama," she shot back.

"How's life?"

"Fair," she stated as her son came out back, looking at Glock. He looked back at the kid, trying to see if they had any resemblance.

Olivia shook her head, seeing how Glock was trying to size her son up.

"He's yours, you goofy," she said, shaking her head.

Glock pulled out a gun and shot the kid in the head. Olivia screamed before Glock turned his gun on her.

Boc, Boc, Boc, Boc, Boc...

Glock walked out the crib feeling a little bad, but he didn't think Olivia's son was his when she first had him. He also saw her with

Kazzy a couple of weeks ago, and that's what sent him over the edge.

***

Norfolk, VA

Gotti called Uncle Slim and Knight to his mini mansion for a small get together.

"I wonder why he called me up here," Knight asked Uncle Slim, who shrugged his shoulders, as both men were in their thoughts.

Knight and Stephen had been doing a lot of under the table drug transactions and having a strong affair. Knight had no clue she was also married until after he had sex with her. One thing Knight was against was fucking with married women.

"Men, have a seat, thanks for coming out," Gotti greeted both of them as they walked into the crib, which was polished.

"Gotti, what's up?" Uncle Slim asked, sitting down.

"I have good news," said Gotti.

"What's that?" Knight asked, hoping Gotti didn't know about him and Stephen's business transaction.

"I found out we have a rat in our circle." Gotti passed Knight some paper.

"Good, let's kill him!" Uncle Slim shouted.

"Come to find out, he's been working for dem people trying to bring down my empire. I want Knight to take care of this issue," Gotti directed.

Knight was reading the papers, shocked to see the name on the paper.

"Let me see that shit." Uncle Slim was ready for war, he hated rats.

When he saw his name and statements willing to work for the feds to get out of jail early, he wanted to cry.

"Damn, Slim, you turned on me." Gotti pulled out a gun as six goons walked in the room with assault rifles.

Uncle Slim's face said it all.

"I'm sorry..."

"Shhhh... Knight, your uncle was about to give you up too. He got out too early from prison, so I did my research and came to find out, our boy is an agent. That's not all. I know you been doing business with my little sister, but don't let her pretty looks fool you," Gotti said, handing Knight a weapon.

"That was only business, nothing personal." Knight stared at his uncle, who was sweating bullets.

"I knew, but both of you not leaving here tonight, and the choice is up to you, Knight." Gotti stared at Slim, thinking about everything he'd done for him.

Knight looked at the gun then at his uncle, and fired two shots into his head with no remorse. Knight couldn't believe his uncle was about to set him up just for a time cut.

"Good job, Knight. Consider the news of you and my sister long gone. Let's focus on this money. I like your style, so I'ma give you all of Slim's areas to run how you please," Gotti told him.

"Aight." Knight handed Gotti the gun back, leaving.

Chapter 34

River Park Towers, Bronx

DayDay was in his apartment placing the last brick inside the suitcase in preparation to meet with his uncle. Selling drugs was all DayDay knew since he was sixteen years old. His older brother, Moon, lived in New Jersey and he was a big-time dope boy.

DayDay had River Park Towers on lock with the crack game. He had fourteen workers in the projects making at least five thousand dollars a day. At twenty-one years old, DayDay's plan was to retire by next year and move to Miami on the beach.

Not too many people knew about DayDay because he was a low-key hustler. He didn't wear jewelry or drive fancy cars. DayDay learned from his pops, who was a big-time kingpin in the Bronx in the 90s. His pops was doing a life sentence for drugs, but it was because of his luxury lifestyle of buying mansions, fancy clothes, and expensive cars.

DayDay placed the suitcase under the living room table next to his gun, a loaded MP5. Looking out the peephole at solstice, he saw his uncle Rags standing there with sweat on his shiny bald head.

His uncle Rags showed him the game his first day off the porch, and that's why he kept him with him at all times, especially while traveling. When DayDay opened the door, a man appeared behind his uncle with a gun to Uncle Rags' head.

"Get on the floor, son," Less told his cousin DayDay as he did what Less told him.

"Less, that's crazy, bro, we family," Uncle Rags stated in a hurtful tone.

"Nigga, we ain't family."

Boc, Boc, Boc...

Less shot Uncle Rags in the head then went to DayDay, who was his first cousin.

"DayDay, where the drugs? Don't make this harder than it gotta be, brotty," Less told DayDay who was sobbing, watching the blood pour out his uncle's head.

"Under the living room table. Less, don't kill me. I got shit to live for, bro. I never crossed you, cuz, word up, son." DayDay was hoping he could talk some sense into his cousin, who he never fucked with because his brother D Fatal Brim robbed and shot his brother in New Jersey.

"Get your bitch ass up and go get the shit." Less let DayDay get up and walk into the living room.

Less didn't see the MP5 behind the suitcase under the table. DayDay tried his hand and reached for the MP5 assault rifle. Luckily, Less saw the gun barrel in the ceiling mirror and fired four shots into DayDay's backside, kicking him over the table.

"Ahhhhhh..." DayDay's frail body flew across the room.

Boc, Boc, Boc...

Less fired three shots into his cousin's face, then took the suitcase and left.

***

Outside, Less snuck through the side lot. It was dark out, so Less rocked a black hoodie to blend in with the darkness.

Bloc, Bloc, Bloc...

Less turned around to see YG a few feet behind him shooting like a mad man, trying to take his head while he ran for cover.

Behind a Honda truck, Less put the suitcase down and sent three shots back, stopping YG in his tracks making him get low. Less looked over his shoulder and saw two other shooters coming on his right side. He had to think of something quick, but nothing came to mind.

Boc, Boc, Boc, Boc...

Less shot one of the gunmen in the middle of his chest. YG sent a drum roll of shots at Less, making him dip off the next row of cars, climbing in a car, driving out the lot with the lights off, flying over speedbumps.

***

Union Ave, Bronx

Glock leaned into Cherly's luscious body and eased his way between her parted thick and chocolate thighs.

"Yessss, uhmmmmmmm," Cherly moaned as he went deeper in her tight kitty, opening her walls further. Glock slid back and rammed deep until he hit the bottom of her womanhood, repeating this process, sending her over the edge.

"Uhhggggg! Fuck, Glock," she moaned, trying to fuck his dick back while sucking on his lips as he fucked the life outta her in missionary.

Cheryl was a short, dark skin, thick beauty with short hair, and the baby mother of his best friend, Bankroll. Glock and Bankroll had a falling out over some money, now Glock was fucking his baby mother.

When they were done, juices were left all over the bed where Bankroll slept with Cheryl every night.

Romell Tukes

Chapter 35

Fairfax, VA
One Month Later

Gotti had a large, beautiful mansion in a gated community, surrounded by the woods and his own private lake. It was getting late and Gotti was in his office doing his taxes, getting everything together to send out to the IRS in Austin, TX.

With over ten businesses, Gotti was getting so much money he had five stash houses all across VA. Since killing Slim, he'd been on the low because he knew the people Slim was reporting to wanted answers, but Slim's body was somewhere deep in the ocean.

Gotti couldn't believe it when he heard his close friend was a rat trying to back him. When he saw the paperwork, he knew it was true and Slim left him no choice. Never had Gotti thought out of all people, it would be Slim to cross him.

Knight had been taking over the city of Norfolk. Gotti was proud of the youngin'. He had a strong liking for him. He saw something in him that reminded him of himself when he was new in the game.

Gotti heard gunshots coming from inside his house. He ran out of his private office to see his guards in a gun battle with eight shooters using high-power assault rifles.

A toe-to-toe gun battle wasn't Gotti's cup of tea, so he went into his hideout, which was behind a double glass mirror in the hallway. To go in the safe room, he had to go into the hallway closet, pull a latch on the wall, and crawl into a small entrance.

***

Knight saw one of his men hit the floor.

Tat-tat-tat-tat-tat-tat-tat...

Knight shot two of the guards, running from wall to wall. With two men down, he had six left, and Gotti had three goons left.

"To your left, Knight!" one of Knight's soldiers yelled, shooting one of Gotti's men trying to get a clean shot on him from the top of the stairs.

Tat-tat-tat-tat-tat-tat-tat-tat...

The big muscle head with dreads rolled down the stairs. The other two guards popped out shooting from the living room area where they were hiding under the bar counter.

Tat-tat-tat-tat-tat-tat-tat...

Two more of Knight's soldiers got hit up, dying instantly. Knight and the rest of his men killed the last of Gotti's army.

"Search the house!" Knight shouted, making his way upstairs, looking for Gotti while his crew searched for drugs.

***

Gotti was in the small panic room looking out the mirror, listening to the footsteps, wondering who was trying to kill him. Sweat dripped down his forehead and under his arms. He thought about calling Knight, but if he pulled out his phone, the light would be seen from the other side of the mirror.

When he saw Knight stop in front of the mirror, Gotti couldn't believe it. Knight looked at himself and kept walking, searching the rooms for Gotti.

***

Knight checked every room and saw no signs of Gotti, which made him upset.

"Yo, Knight!" Paco yelled from downstairs.

"Yooo..."

"We got everything, we out!" Paco shouted.

Knight made his way back downstairs to see Kazzy Loc and Paco with four trash bags full of money and bricks.

"Damn." Knight smiled.

"He had all this in the kitchen cabinet, cuz," Kazzy stated.

Knight brought his brother and crew down, except Less and Black, they stayed in New York.

150

Knight had been plotting on Gotti since he first met him. There was a perfect chance to rise to the top, and Knight wasn't going to miss the ride. He still planned to stay in Norfolk, VA and continue to get money. He'd built a small army under his command, so he was ready for war.

***

Mill Brook Projects, BX

Paco and Kazzy rode in two different cars back to New York with Hasley and Mauda, to make it look like a road trip. One car carried the drugs and the other car carried the money.

Paco had Hasley and Mauda go to the crib to split up the money for the guys. Knight already took his cut when they were in VA.

Black and Less called Kazzy, telling him to come to the hood, ASAP. It was an emergency.

"I hope this ain't no dumb shit, cuz, word to the gang," Kazzy told Paco as they hopped out the rental SUV to see Black and Less approach them.

"Yo, son, we need to talk. It's some shit going on around here," Less spoke up, looking at all three men.

"Speak, nigga," Paco said.

"Two of our spots got hit, both on Burnside," Black said.

"What!" Kazzy yelled.

"Factz, but that's not it, son. Wild niggas been getting robbed all around the city, bro," Less said.

"Shit, we gotta get Glock, boy doing too much," Kazzy stated.

"How we know it's Glock? It could be anybody," Paco said.

"We gonna find out," Less said strongly.

Chapter 36

Queens, NY
Three Weeks Later

Glock was in the strip club watching the exotic dancers slide up and down the pole, shaking their asses like there was no tomorrow. There was one dancer Glock had been watching all night, a sexy bitch with a crazy body.

He was sippin' on D'ussé, bopping his head to the music trying to clear his thought process because a couple of his spots recently got robbed in the South Bronx. The robberies left four of his foot soldiers dead and 200 keys overall taken.

Glock knew Kazzy and his crew had to do it, because they were still at war. Nobody else in the state of New York would have the balls to rob Glock.

The stripper Glock had been eyeing all night made her way into his section and just started dancing on his dick. Glock saw the nice little puff of titties she had while bending over. He felt her phat kitty, which was extra wet.

She turned around and dropped between his legs, undoing his pants. Glock was so horny he was about to bust out his pants. The stripper jerked his pole, spitting on it then kissing the head with her full, phat lips.

Without him paying attention, the woman spit a razor out her mouth and slashed Glock across his face. His face split open from his ear to his lip.

"Ahhhhhhhhh, bitch!" Glock yelled as Hasley ran off like a track star. By the time his guards came to his aid, blood was all over the VIP area.

Hasley was working tonight, and when she saw Glock staring at her, she seduced him with her body.

She knew Paco would be proud of her. She only wished she had her gun on her, but it was in the car. Driving back home, she thought about her late friend, Katty, she missed. Mauda lived with her and Paco, and she was cool, but she wasn't close to Katty.

***

Uptown, Bronx

Black was driving around thinking about his mom and little brother, Blu, who he hadn't seen since their mom's funeral. It was almost 12 pm and he hadn't eaten shit all day, so he was starving. He pulled over at a Crown Fried Chicken before he made his way to his mom's tombstone, then he had to go see Paco in Parkchester.

Black walked in the chicken spot and saw a couple of niggas in line with red flags representing the Blood gang. Beef was so crazy in the town, Black ain't trust no Bloods except his Mackballers crew.

After ordering his food, Black stepped outside and ran into YG coming up the block. Both men pulled out and started shooting right on the sidewalk.

Bloc, Bloc, Bloc, Bloc, Bloc, Bloc, Bloc...

YG shot Black in the side, dropping him, while the police sped down the block. YG wanted to finish Black but he wasn't trying to go back to jail. He was already out on bail. YG ran up the block, cutting through side blocks, losing the cops. The police found Black crawling away from the gun he had while blood leaked out his side. Medical pulled up and helped Black, putting pressure on his wound until they got him in the EMT truck, taking him to the local hospital.

***

Jacoby Hospital, BX
Next Day

Black was told he was being charged with a shooting and a gun charge, which was sending him on a first-class trip to Rikers Island Jail. Black laid in the hospital bed next to two NYPD cops, who were ready to take him to jail.

Today was the worst day of his life so far, besides losing his mom. He was shot and going to jail. He knew his day couldn't get any worse. Just when Black closed his eyes, the hospital room door opened.

"Mr. Woodberry, I'm Homicide Detective Russle and I would like to question you about three murders, if you don't mind," the older white man asked, looking at a folder then to Black.

"You arresting me?"

"No, not yet at least. I'm trying to cut you a break because your mother was my partner for a very long time, and I owe her this," the detective said seriously.

"How about I don't know shit and go swallow a dick," Black shot back.

"Have it your way, tough guy." The detective walked out.

Black couldn't believe they were on him for three bodies. He was sick, and the room was starting to spin.

"That's a hell of a long time in jail, kid," one of the NYPD officers in the room said.

Chapter 37

Mott Haven, Bronx
One Month Later

Today, Mott Haven was having a big party in the projects for the hood's fallen soldiers, especially PG.

It was dark out now, and the back of the projects was starting to die as people went back to their hood or home. Free weed and liquor was flowing all through the projects.

YG and a gang of young gunnerz were posted up, talking and hanging out, taking pics for their niggas in jail and for social media.

"Where Killer Gz at, bro? I saw him earlier today," Thuggy asked.

"He in Harlem with the guys," YG said, taking a long pull of loud.

"Yo, ma, come here!" one of the dudes yelled, standing on the bench seeing five females walk past as a group, looking like snacks.

"Niggas trying to slide to the Heights tonight, bro. We need some more of that OG KUSH, and they got a mean after party on Dyckman," Loony G'z stated, drinking Henny out the bottle, feeling the effects.

"I'm down, bro," YG said, texting his Dominican chick from the Heights.

***

"Yo, son, my ass hurt. We been out here since noon. I'm ready to turn this shit up," Paco said, pointing his Draco out the car window.

"It's too many of them niggas out there, just wait ten minutes, bro. Niggas is separating out," Kazzy Loc said, watching the packed park behind the playground and buildings.

Shit had been low key in Mill Brook Park. The money flowing was crazy. Since their spots got robbed, they bounced back twenty times harder. Since the VA move, life had been a blessing.

Everybody was driving foreign luxury cars and buying houses outside of the Bronx.

The only person who wasn't out to enjoy the money and freedom was Black, who was still locked up on Rikers Island.

Kazzy saw a couple of niggas go in the buildings.

"We litty, bro." Kazzy grabbed his AR-15 assault rifle from the backseat of the Mustang.

***

YG and six of his homies shared four bottles of Henny, something they did on the regular.

"Malik wrote me last night. He's locked up in Kentucky, son," Phil Gz told everybody, puffing on loud.

Tat-tat-tat-tat-tat-tat-tat-tat-tat-tat-tat-tat-tat-tat-tat-tat-tat...

Paco and Kazzy lit up the projects like it was lights, camera, action. YG and his crew were taking cover while trying to shoot back, but the assault rifle's 223 bullets were chopping them down.

Niggas were coming out the building to help, but when they saw all the gunfire, they thought different and posted in the lobby.

Bloc, Bloc, Bloc, Bloc...

Tat-tat-tat-tat-tat-tat-tat-tat...

Most of YG's guys were laying in pools of blood, and he was also shot in his thigh. He hid on the side of a garbage can reloading his gun, seeing his man across from him fire at Paco, who was letting his Draco rip.

Tat-tat-tat-tat-tat-tat...

When YG saw Phil Gz's head explode, he popped up shooting on his good leg.

Bloc, Bloc, Bloc, Bloc, Bloc...

YG ran in the closest building with his good leg, getting away while six of his childhood friends laid dead outside.

***

Norfolk, VA

Knight was on his way to drop off the last ten keys he had in his car under his seat. His boy, Duke Boy, was driving the car on a small bridge on his way to Hampton.

Within two hours, Knight sold 100 keys and he was buying drugs from Gotti's sister, who he was going out of VA to meet.

"You sure your cousin and them is good people, bro? I don't be dealing with no niggas," Knight stated, laid back in the leather seats of the newest Audi.

"Yeah, dawg, I'm telling you, folk, my kin good, solid people," Duke Boy said, seeing two cop cars flashing red and blue lights.

"What the fuck..." Knight looked out the back windows to see cop cars on their ass. He felt the car slowing up.

"Nigga, drive!" Knight rolled down the windows, grabbing keys from under the seats, busting them open and tossing them out the window in the ocean under the bridge.

By the time he got to his last one, a police car rammed into the Audi, making it spin out of control. Knight's head slammed into the dashboard before the Audi came to a complete stop and the police surrounded them. The police snatched them out of the car and arrested them, finding one key of coke and two handguns with 30-shot clips.

***

Arlington Jail, VA

Knight was sent straight to the county jail with no medical attention or nothing. When the police found out Knight was from New York, they thought they hit the motherload.

Knight found out Duke Boy set him up. The whole time, he was working for the police lining him up. Sitting in the bullpen, he was already homesick, missing his crew, mom, sister, and Bronx lifestyle.

He regretted coming down south with these hating ass country niggas. He knew if he had a bail he would call Kazzy, who had Gotti's sister's number. If Kazzy couldn't get him out, he knew for a fact she could. Plus, he had money scattered all over VA.

Chapter 38

Rikers Island Jail, Queens

Black's bail bondsman posted bail this morning, so he was free to go home and keep up with his court dates, or he could come back for bail jumping.

While locked up, he got into two fist fights, and he came out on top because he used to be a boxer when he was younger.

The guards were escorting Black out of the prison, and he was so happy, he wanted to dance and roll around on the floor like a little kid. At the gate, there were two all-black tinted SUV trucks with six federal agents leaning on the outside.

Black wasn't worried about them, he was looking for a cab to take him to the Bronx.

"Mr. Woodberry, we need you to come with us. You're under arrest for murder," one of the federal agents said, pulling out his cuffs placing them on Black.

"Y'all got the wrong nigga!" Black shouted as they tossed him in their truck, pulling off on their way to a Manhattan federal building in the cut.

***

An Hour Later

Black couldn't believe what was going on. He felt like this was a joke. He was being charged with murder and two attempted murders.

"You look like there is something on your mind," the agent stated, tapping his pen on the notepad.

"I ain't do this shit."

"Well, if you can't tell us who did, then you're going to be taking the charge," the agent replied.

"This shit won't hold up at trial. Y'all got nothing on me, man. I ain't do this shit!" Black shouted, cuffed to the table.

"It's going to stick good, we got too much shit on you. We're working on some more murders you and your crew did, unless you can give us them."

"So, I will walk straight out the door if I tell you who did all of this shit?" Black asked, in deep thought.

"Yeap." The agent smiled because they didn't really have anything on him.

"Ok, but I want an agreement."

"Sure, I'll be right back." The agent left and came right back with some fake papers.

Black told him everything about Knight and Kazzy. He told on over ten bodies.

***

Bare Hill Prison, NY

"Big Blazer, that dumb nigga, Ant, talking about he want you to pull up on him," PR said, approaching his big homie.

Big Blazer was the biggest nigga on the yard at 6'5 and three hundred pounds of solid muscle. He was from the Soundview section of the Bronx. They called him Big Blazer because he was a Sex, Money, Murder gang member with a lot of status.

Big Blazer was Glock's big homie and his childhood friend. With a couple of months left, Big Blazer was happy his bid was over because he'd been through a lot of shit.

"Where boy at?"

"On the basketball court," PR told Big Blazer, who stopped his chess game and got up, walking on the grass with seven of his homies.

When niggas saw walking on the court, everything stopped.

"Yo, Big Blazer, I was—"

Whack!!

Big Blazer cut the young man's sentence off by knocking him out on the court, leaving everybody amazed. His soldier dragged Ant's body off the court. The basketball game continued, and Big Blazer went back to his chess game. Big Blazer hated when he had to tell a nigga to go on a mission and he tried to talk his way out of it like Ant did.

Prison was Big Blazer's life story. Being in and out these cages burnt him out, he just wanted to get some money and stay outta jail. Since he'd been locked up, Glock was there supporting him every step of the way while everybody turned their backs on him.

Exercising, reading, and studying was all Big Blazer did to maintain his sanity in the belly of the beast.

***

Washington Heights, NY

Gwyneth and her mother, Angie, were at the corner store where the Dominicans sold fruit and fresh vegetables. Gwyneth was beautiful for a woman in her early forties. She was Paco's aunt and Angie was his grandma.

They both raised Paco and his two sisters since birth. Paco took good care of his family and they never questioned his lifestyle, they just told him to go to church. Angie was old school and she was a loyal, devoted Roman Catholic.

Once inside the building, they saw a man waiting at the elevator.

"Hey," Gwyneth said, never seeing the man before around the area, but she was very respectful to everybody.

When the elevator door opened, the man held it open for them.

"What a gentleman," Angie stated as she and Gwyneth walked inside.

The man pulled out a 9mm Taurus.

Boc, Boc, Boc, Boc, Boc, Boc...

YG gave both women head shots then ran out the building, praying nobody was outside to witness his face.

The last two days, he'd been hiding out in the Heights. Last night, he was going to the corner store to buy some Dutches and a pack of Newports. He saw Paco walking both women into the building, so since then, he'd been stalking the building waiting on the time to make his move.

Chapter 39

Arlington, VA

Knight was still in Arlington County Jail waiting on his next court date. He recently went to court and was denied bail. He was the only New York nigga or outta town nigga in his unit, besides two D.C. niggas who were running around robbing niggas. Knight made a big knife just in case they tried him.

This was Knight's first time really in jail, besides spending a few days in central booking in New York. There was a pull-up and dip bar in the unit, so Knight spent most of his days exercising and reading the Qur'an an old head Muslim brother gave him. Growing up, he was never into religion or gang banging, but reading the Qur'an opened his eyes to a lot of things.

A young, nice, brown-skin, petite CO woman, Ms. Stanford, was coming his way while he was doing pull-ups, 30 reps a set. She stopped and watched his back muscles flex, blushing.

"You have a visit. Where you from? Someone told me you was from New York," she asked while staring at his body.

Knight knew how VA women loved New York niggas, so he loved stunting on them country niggas. Almost every inmate tried to holler at Ms. Stanford, but she didn't give nobody no play, not even the corny ass guards.

"It depends on who's asking." Knight looked around to see close to sixty-something inmates staring at him.

"I'm asking. You so quiet," she said in her country accent.

"I'm sure you can look me up and find out where I'm from."

"I already did, just wanted to hear you talk. Enjoy your visit," she told him, walking off throwing her little booty.

Knight went to clean himself up and get ready for his visit.

***

Knight thought it was a lawyer visit from his public defender. He hadn't been in touch with Kazzy or his men yet, because he wanted to see if the feds were coming, because anytime someone got caught with a gun and drugs, they were most likely to end up in the feds.

Walking past a couple of visitors, Knight couldn't believe who was sitting there looking more beautiful than ever.

"Stephen, what are you doing here?" He sat down across from her, looking at her beautiful smile.

"Damn, nigga, can a bitch show some love and support? It's not all about sex, even though I would like to... I'll save that for another visit, but how you holding up?" she asked, getting serious.

"I'm ok, hoping the feds don't come."

"Nah, you good on that, trust me. I know people that know people. I'm glad you can hold water. I got a lot of respect for you, because a lot of people love biting cheese," she said in disgust.

"I'd rather do pushups in a cell before I rat, big facts."

"I know, but I got you the best lawyer in VA, and my people should be putting money on your books right now. I'ma pop up on you every now and then. I say the most you gotta do is 2-4 years. The kid Duke Boy was found dead a couple of days ago," she said, giving him a wink.

"Thanks for everything," Knight said, seeing she was ready to leave.

"I gotta fly out to Vegas. I'll be in touch." She kissed him on his cheek and left. Knight never saw a chick so real.

***

Highbridge, BX

YG's mom was leaving her job at a daycare she just started working at last month. Her son just called her telling her he bought her a house. She couldn't believe it, because living in Mott Haven was hell. It was loud, dirty, and the violence was crazy.

After burying her son, PG, and her daughter in the same year, she feared what would happen next. YG was all she had left, and she prayed every night he would leave the street life alone for his own good.

Walking towards her car, a Honda with tints pulled up on her and rolled down the passenger window. Thinking it was a friend or one of her co-workers, she stopped and looked inside.

Boc, Boc, Boc, Boc, Boc, Boc, Boc...

The bullets pierced her heart and lungs, sending her a few feet back, crashing into the pavement.

The Honda drove off. Paco was happy his little cousin went to the same daycare she worked at. Hasley drove off to Webster to pick up Mauda.

***

Staten Island, NY

Black was hiding out in a rundown apartment full of mice, rats, and roaches, sniffing coke and smoking wet. The feds were trying to build a case on his guys, and he was the star witness.

Black was having thoughts of backing out of his agreement, but he didn't want to go to jail. He felt like a bitch nigga because his crew always had his back and kept it solid with him. Black laid on the couch high off PCP, in his own mind, confused.

Romell Tukes

Chapter 40

Westchester, NY

Bankroll was a new patient in a drug rehab center. He recently overdosed on prescription pills and lean. He was sitting in a group listening to other drug users' stories, shocked at a lot of things he heard. He knew there was no way he could continue to live like an addict to swallow his pain.

Bankroll found out Glock and his baby mother were a couple now, and that crushed his heart to the max! Losing family and friends for Glock made him hate Glock. If he knew Glock was a snake, he would have played him close and carried him like a fuck nigga.

***

Mill Brook Projects, BX
A Month Later

Mrs. Wilson was leaving her crib on her way to a doctor's appointment across town. She'd recently found out she had breast cancer, but she hadn't found the right time to tell her kids.

Kazzy was running the streets, Knight was out of town somewhere, and her daughter was in college. Her younger son, Lil' K, was the one she got to see daily because he was always home.

She got in the back lot, which was full of snow because there was a snowstorm.

"Shit," she mumbled, stepping in the snow trying not to slip.

When she made it to her G-Wagon Benz SUV, a man in a peacoat hopped out the GMC truck on the side of her.

"You Kazzy's mom?"

"Sorry, do I know you? And what you want wit' my son?" she asked, ready to curse him out.

BOOM...

Glock laid a bullet between her eyes, leaving her body in a snow pile. He'd been waiting all morning to catch Kazzy's mom coming out the building.

There was a crazy snow storm, so Glock knew the police would take a while to get there.

***

Gun Hill Projects, BX
Four Days Later

Kazzy was laying low, trying to get his mind back in the right place after losing Olivia and his mom. He knew something had to give after losing his mom. He ain't hear from none of his brothers in months, and he had no clue where they were at.

Kazzy was at a Jamaican chick's crib smoking heavy weed while Paco and Less controlled the streets. Nobody knew what happened to Black. It was like he fell off the surface of the earth. He felt something was extremely wrong.

"You good, daddy?" a super thick, high-yellow complexioned woman said, walking out the bathroom in boy shorts and a short tank top.

"Yeah, ma, I'm straight. I'm about up outta here," Knight told her, getting out.

She wanted to keep Knight locked down as long as she could, because the way he was murdering her love box, she was in love.

"When you coming back?" she asked, to get no reply, only a door slam.

***

Arlington Jail, VA
Three Months Later

Knight was leaving his visit he had with a woman he met a while back in New York, named Mita. When he saw the sexy woman, he couldn't believe it. Last time he saw Mita, she was on her way to becoming a lawyer.

170

Mita told him she moved to VA and saw him on tv months ago. She took his name and looked him up to see he was close, so she came to visit. She recently became a DA in Dale City Court. Knight was shocked but made sure he didn't talk about his case.

The vibe was so strong between them, she wanted to come once a week. She told him since his case was caught in a different county, she couldn't help him. Luckily, Stephen paid $300,000 for the lawyer in VA and D.C. Even Mita knew who the lawyer was, since his name was big in the court system.

Knight was still mourning over his mother's loss that took a toll on him, but he knew he had to remain strong while in his situation.

Two days ago, Knight fucked CO Stanford in the CO bathroom in the hallway on the third floor. Her shit was dripping. Knight never had no pussy like hers and he was addicted, but so was she.

When he made it back to the cell, everybody was standing around chilling, talking, or about to use the pay phone to call their family.

Knight saw a couple of niggas staring at him while he made his way back to his cell. Knight hated this unit because niggas were too nosey and sneaky. He didn't trust none of them country niggas. There were only two niggas he dealt with, and they were from Bad News, VA.

When he was about to take a piss, three niggas ran in his cell with knives, attacking him. Knight had his knife under his bed, but by the time he made it to his knife, he was stabbed 17 times in his back. Knight stabbed one of the men in his face and one his stomach, but they were getting off on him. The door flew open and a nigga from Bad News stabbed two of the men in the side, helping Knight. The police came and sprayed mace into the cell, placing cuffs on everybody, taking all five men to the hospital for their stab wounds. One man almost didn't make it.

Romell Tukes

Chapter 41

Richmond, VA

Gotti was in his other mansion surrounded by thirty goons all throughout the $13.4 million palace. After what happened in his last mansion, Gotti refused to be caught slipping again.

He thought about that event every night. Seeing Knight ambush his crib killing his men had Gotti on some other shit. Gotti walked around the house with his pistol, not taking any chances.

He put 100,000 dollars on Knight's head in Arlington County Jail. When he saw Knight on the news one night, he knew it was time to put a plan together. One of his client's brother was locked up with Knight on the same unit, so he and two other men took the money and went to put in some work.

Gotti heard Knight was still alive because a nigga from Bad News jumped in, and he was pissed off about that.

"Gotti, your company has arrived. He's clean," one of his security guards told him while Gotti was in his bar area pouring a glass of Patrón.

"Aight." Gotti saw Fats walking into the living room with his big smile.

"Bossman, what's up." Fats gave Gotti a big hug.

Gotti was Fats' plug, and when Fats recently heard Knight was in VA, he called Gotti to tell him about Knight. To Fats' surprise, Gotti knew who Knight was and he wanted him dead also.

"You getting skinny," Gotti told Fats with a laugh.

"Ain't no way I'm getting skinny, I'm eating too good. Maybe your eyes getting small," Fats stated, sitting on the leather couch taking off his designer shoes, putting his feet on Gotti's table.

The relationship these men shared was more than business. Fats met Gotti when he was living in VA in his younger days, and since then, they remained cool and formed a bond.

"I can't believe this little fucker been in VA the whole time. My worker killed his mom a couple of months ago. I know that touched his soul." Fats started laughing.

"We gotta get him and his crew out the picture. We gotta take care of all of them, or it will bite us on the ass. It's clear they knew a lot about us," said Gotti.

"Yeah, but they don't know we deal with each other, so we got the upper hand," Fats stated seriously, getting up to go make himself a drink.

"I just want those niggas dead, but you ready to get down to business?" Gotti asked, ready to talk money.

***

Pelham, Bronx

Paco was in the crib watching a TV show on DirecTV. Hasley just left to go pick up dinner from a Spanish restaurant they ordered food from daily.

Since his grandma and auntie were killed, Paco had been trying to hunt Glock down, but he was nowhere to be found. Paco's grandmom and aunt raised him and his sisters, so burying them was like burying himself.

"I'm glad we can spend some time alone, papi," Mauda said, kissing his lips while they cuddled under the blanket on the living room sofa.

"You don't like Hasley? Because the way you was eating her ass, it's hard to tell," Paco told her, making her laugh, because their sex was crazy.

"It's not that, I just like sucking your dick when it's us. I can get into it more," she said.

"Shit, I'm not complaining." He laughed.

"I'ma grab a soda." She got up and went inside the kitchen while Paco finished watching TV.

"Babe, grab me a soda!" Paco yelled, then he felt cold steel to the back of his head.

"I'm sorry, Paco, but Glock's brother, Dollar, sent me, and I love my husband dearly," she stated.

174

"Handle your business, little bitch. I'll see you in hell, ma." Paco was calm, ready to die.

Boc, Boc, Boc...

Paco looked behind him to see Mauda's body collapse. Hasley was behind her with a smoking gun with tears in her eyes.

Hasley forgot her wallet in the room, so she had to turn around and come back. When she saw Mauda with a gun to Paco's head, she wasted no time blowing her head off.

"We gotta get outta here, baby," Paco told Hasley, going to the back room to get anything that could lead Mauda's murder back to them. Paco knew Hasley was his ride or die bitch to the casket. He even thought about marrying her.

***
New Jersey

Glock had been in New Jersey for the past couple of weeks trying to open up shop in Jersey City. The Bronx was too hot. The feds were booking a lot of gangs, even in his hood, but Glock couldn't go out like that.

He was in a nice condo with Bankroll's baby mother, who he couldn't get rid of. She was in the kitchen cooking dinner when the front door flew open.

BOOM!

Tat-Tat-Tat-Tat-Tat-Tat...

"Ahhhhhhh, bitch!" Glock yelled in pain, feeling bullets rip through his legs as he fell out the dining room chair.

Bankroll's baby mother came out of the kitchen and was hit with ten hollow-tip bullets to her breast.

"I got money, drugs, whatever y'all need, fam, in the Lexus coupe trunk outside. Please, I won't never come back to Jersey, I swear," Glock cried, seeing the two young men look at each other with a smirk.

"I hate bitch niggas," Lil' K said before he shot Glock fourteen times in his face.

Lil' K and Bugatti Boy had been watching Glock's condo for a week now. When Lil' K heard Glock killed his mom, he was on a manhunt since Kazzy was too focused on whatever he was focused on.

"We gotta get back to the town, bro. Red and Banger just hit me saying everything in place," Bugatti Boy said, walking out the apartment.

Lil' K and his crew had been the ones robbing everybody around the Bronx, even his own brother's spots, but Lil' K didn't care. Kazzy was all for self.

It was the takeover for Lil' K and his gang, and since losing his mom, his mind was ruthless, and he was on some *anybody can get it* shit.

***

Webster Projects, Bronx

Less was leaving the building where two of his workers were upstairs busting down bricks and bagging up, which was an all-night process.

Outside the building, he saw a sexy young exotic chick in some jeans and timbs, smoking a cigarette.

Less knew she was younger, but she was a bad little bitch. He knew it wasn't creep shit to ask her age, or her name at least.

"How old are you, ma? Because you out here looking good," Less told her face to face, even gone off how sexy she was up close.

"What?" she asked.

When he was about to repeat himself, a long, thick metal pipe slammed into the back of his head, knocking him out. The chick and two men dragged his body to the van parked on the curb with the sliding door open.

***

High Points, Bronx

Twenty Minutes Later

Less was hog tied with zip ties and saw two young niggas laughing at him, with the sexy chick he saw standing in front of the projects.

"Who are you?"

"We ain't gonna entertain you, bro," Blu stated.

"You Black's brother?" Less asked Blu.

"Nigga, I'm Blu. I'm my own man, son, but you worried about the wrong thing, bro," Blu told him.

The warehouse doors opened and two niggas walked inside.

"I know that's not the illest nigga in the Bronx," Lil' K stated, walking towards Less in the abandoned warehouse.

"Lil' K, I can't believe you violated like this, bro, we family, son!" Less shouted.

"Nah, son, we not family. You and my brothers are family, this my family." Lil' K looked at his crew who all had assault rifles out.

"So y'all been the niggas robbing everybody?" Less asked.

"Factz," Banger replied, standing next to his sister, Red, who Less tried to bag.

"So, what now? If you gonna kill me, let's get it over with," Less said, sounding like a real G.

"Ohhh, we gonna get there, we're just waiting on our guest," Lil' K said laughing, rolling a blunt of bud.

***

Jackson Projects, BX

Kazzy just picked up $200,000 from his man, Lil' Proud. Kazzy had been focused on a bag and finding Glock, but he was a ghost just like Black.

There was a lot of funny shit going on with everybody, and Kazzy didn't know who to trust. He found out Knight was locked up in VA. He just wrote him and sent him a large amount of money.

Kazzy saw a little note on his windshield, and he was about to get rid of it until he saw his name on it.

He read the note, which said:

Come to 179 in Hunts Points in forty minutes or Less is dead and you're next. Bring 200 keys and 700,000 in cash...Lil' K.

When Kazzy saw his little brother's name, he thought it was a joke, but he knew it wasn't. Kazzy was upset that his own blood crossed him like this. Now it was starting to add up who was jacking his spots.

Kazzy went to go get the drugs and money to pay for his big homie's life, but this was the beginning of a new war...

To Be Continued...
Jack Boyz N Da Bronx 2
Coming Soon

Submission Guideline

Submit the first three chapters of your completed manuscript to ldpsubmissions@gmail.com, subject line: Your book's title. The manuscript must be in a .doc file and sent as an attachment. Document should be in Times New Roman, double spaced and in size 12 font. Also, provide your synopsis and full contact information. If sending multiple submissions, they must each be in a separate email.

Have a story but no way to send it electronically? You can still submit to LDP/Ca$h Presents. Send in the first three chapters, written or typed, of your completed manuscript to:

LDP: Submissions Dept
Po Box 944
Stockbridge, Ga 30281

DO NOT send original manuscript. Must be a duplicate.

Provide your synopsis and a cover letter containing your full contact information.

Thanks for considering LDP and Ca$h Presents.

Coming Soon from Lock Down Publications/Ca$h Presents

BOW DOWN TO MY GANGSTA

By **Ca$h**

TORN BETWEEN TWO

By **Coffee**

THE STREETS STAINED MY SOUL **II**

By **Marcellus Allen**

BLOOD OF A BOSS **VI**

SHADOWS OF THE GAME II

TRAP BASTARD II

By **Askari**

LOYAL TO THE GAME **IV**

By **T.J. & Jelissa**

IF LOVING YOU IS WRONG… **III**

By **Jelissa**

TRUE SAVAGE **VIII**

MIDNIGHT CARTEL IV

DOPE BOY MAGIC IV

CITY OF KINGZ III

By **Chris Green**

BLAST FOR ME **III**

A SAVAGE DOPEBOY III

CUTTHROAT MAFIA III

DUFFLE BAG CARTEL VI

HEARTLESS GOON VI

By **Ghost**

A HUSTLER'S DECEIT III

KILL ZONE **II**

BAE BELONGS TO ME III

Jack Boyz N Da Bronx

Romell Tukes

KINGPIN DREAMS III
By Paper Boi Rari
CREAM II
By Yolanda Moore
SON OF A DOPE FIEND III
By Renta
FOREVER GANGSTA II
GLOCKS ON SATIN SHEETS III
By Adrian Dulan
LOYALTY AIN'T PROMISED III
By Keith Williams
THE PRICE YOU PAY FOR LOVE III
By Destiny Skai
I'M NOTHING WITHOUT HIS LOVE II
SINS OF A THUG II
By Monet Dragun
LIFE OF A SAVAGE IV
MURDA SEASON IV
GANGLAND CARTEL IV
CHI'RAQ GANGSTAS IV
KILLERS ON ELM STREET II
JACK BOYZ N DA BRONX II
By **Romell Tukes**
QUIET MONEY IV
EXTENDED CLIP III
By **Trai'Quan**
THE STREETS MADE ME III
By **Larry D. Wright**
IF YOU CROSS ME ONCE II

182

Jack Boyz N Da Bronx

ANGEL III

By **Anthony Fields**

FRIEND OR FOE III

By **Mimi**

SAVAGE STORMS III

By **Meesha**

BLOOD ON THE MONEY III

By J-Blunt

THE STREETS WILL NEVER CLOSE II

By K'ajji

NIGHTMARES OF A HUSTLA III

By King Dream

IN THE ARM OF HIS BOSS

By Jamila

MONEY, MURDER & MEMORIES III

Malik D. Rice

CONCRETE KILLAZ II

By Kingpen

HARD AND RUTHLESS II

By Von Wiley Hall

LEVELS TO THIS SHYT II

By Ah'Million

MOB TIES II

By SayNoMore

BODYMORE MURDERLAND II

By Delmont Player

THE LAST OF THE OGS II

Tranay Adams

FOR THE LOVE OF A BOSS II

By C. D. Blue

Available Now

RESTRAINING ORDER **I & II**

By **CA$H & Coffee**

LOVE KNOWS NO BOUNDARIES **I II & III**

By **Coffee**

RAISED AS A GOON I, II, III & IV

BRED BY THE SLUMS I, II, III

BLAST FOR ME I & II

ROTTEN TO THE CORE I II III

A BRONX TALE I, II, III

DUFFLE BAG CARTEL I II III IV V

HEARTLESS GOON I II III IV V

A SAVAGE DOPEBOY I II

DRUG LORDS I II III

CUTTHROAT MAFIA I II

By **Ghost**

LAY IT DOWN **I & II**

LAST OF A DYING BREED I II

BLOOD STAINS OF A SHOTTA I & II III

By **Jamaica**

LOYAL TO THE GAME I II III

LIFE OF SIN I, II III

By **TJ & Jelissa**

BLOODY COMMAS I & II

SKI MASK CARTEL I II & III

KING OF NEW YORK I II,III IV V

Jack Boyz N Da Bronx

RISE TO POWER I II III

COKE KINGS I II III IV

BORN HEARTLESS I II III IV

KING OF THE TRAP

By **T.J. Edwards**

IF LOVING HIM IS WRONG...I & II

LOVE ME EVEN WHEN IT HURTS I II III

By **Jelissa**

WHEN THE STREETS CLAP BACK I & II III

THE HEART OF A SAVAGE I II III

By **Jibril Williams**

A DISTINGUISHED THUG STOLE MY HEART I II & III

LOVE SHOULDN'T HURT I II III IV

RENEGADE BOYS I II III IV

PAID IN KARMA I II III

SAVAGE STORMS I II

By **Meesha**

A GANGSTER'S CODE I &, II III

A GANGSTER'S SYN I II III

THE SAVAGE LIFE I II III

CHAINED TO THE STREETS I II III

BLOOD ON THE MONEY I II

By J-Blunt

PUSH IT TO THE LIMIT

By **Bre' Hayes**

BLOOD OF A BOSS **I, II, III, IV, V**

SHADOWS OF THE GAME

TRAP BASTARD

By **Askari**

THE STREETS BLEED MURDER **I, II & III**

Romell Tukes

THE HEART OF A GANGSTA I II& III

By **Jerry Jackson**

CUM FOR ME I II III IV V VI

An **LDP Erotica Collaboration**

BRIDE OF A HUSTLA **I II & II**

THE FETTI GIRLS **I, II& III**

CORRUPTED BY A GANGSTA I, II III, IV

BLINDED BY HIS LOVE

THE PRICE YOU PAY FOR LOVE I II

DOPE GIRL MAGIC I II III

By **Destiny Skai**

WHEN A GOOD GIRL GOES BAD

By **Adrienne**

THE COST OF LOYALTY I II III

By Kweli

A GANGSTER'S REVENGE **I II III & IV**

THE BOSS MAN'S DAUGHTERS I II III IV V

A SAVAGE LOVE **I & II**

BAE BELONGS TO ME I II

A HUSTLER'S DECEIT I, II, III

WHAT BAD BITCHES DO I, II, III

SOUL OF A MONSTER I II III

KILL ZONE

A DOPE BOY'S QUEEN I II

By **Aryanna**

A KINGPIN'S AMBITON

A KINGPIN'S AMBITION **II**

I MURDER FOR THE DOUGH

By **Ambitious**

TRUE SAVAGE I II III IV V VI VII

186

Jack Boyz N Da Bronx

DOPE BOY MAGIC I, II, III
MIDNIGHT CARTEL I II III
CITY OF KINGZ I II
By **Chris Green**
A DOPEBOY'S PRAYER
By **Eddie "Wolf" Lee**
THE KING CARTEL **I, II & III**
By **Frank Gresham**
THESE NIGGAS AIN'T LOYAL **I, II & III**
By **Nikki Tee**
GANGSTA SHYT **I II &III**
By **CATO**
THE ULTIMATE BETRAYAL
By **Phoenix**
BOSS'N UP **I , II & III**
By **Royal Nicole**
I LOVE YOU TO DEATH
By Destiny J
I RIDE FOR MY HITTA
I STILL RIDE FOR MY HITTA
By **Misty Holt**
LOVE & CHASIN' PAPER
By **Qay Crockett**
TO DIE IN VAIN
SINS OF A HUSTLA
By **ASAD**
BROOKLYN HUSTLAZ
By **Boogsy Morina**
BROOKLYN ON LOCK I & II
By **Sonovia**

187

Romell Tukes

GANGSTA CITY
By **Teddy Duke**
A DRUG KING AND HIS DIAMOND I & II III
A DOPEMAN'S RICHES
HER MAN, MINE'S TOO I, II
CASH MONEY HO'S
THE WIFEY I USED TO BE I II
By Nicole Goosby
TRAPHOUSE KING **I II & III**
KINGPIN KILLAZ I II III
STREET KINGS I II
PAID IN BLOOD **I II**
CARTEL KILLAZ I II III
DOPE GODS I II
By **Hood Rich**
LIPSTICK KILLAH **I, II, III**
CRIME OF PASSION I II & III
FRIEND OR FOE I II
By **Mimi**
STEADY MOBBN' **I, II, III**
THE STREETS STAINED MY SOUL
By **Marcellus Allen**
WHO SHOT YA **I, II, III**
SON OF A DOPE FIEND I II
Renta
GORILLAZ IN THE BAY **I II III IV**
TEARS OF A GANGSTA I II
3X KRAZY I II
DE'KARI
TRIGGADALE I II III

Jack Boyz N Da Bronx

Elijah R. Freeman

GOD BLESS THE TRAPPERS I, II, III

THESE SCANDALOUS STREETS I, II, III

FEAR MY GANGSTA I, II, III IV, V

THESE STREETS DON'T LOVE NOBODY I, II

BURY ME A G I, II, III, IV, V

A GANGSTA'S EMPIRE I, II, III, IV

THE DOPEMAN'S BODYGAURD I II

THE REALEST KILLAZ I II III

THE LAST OF THE OGS

Tranay Adams

THE STREETS ARE CALLING

Duquie Wilson

MARRIED TO A BOSS... I II III

By Destiny Skai & Chris Green

KINGZ OF THE GAME I II III IV V

Playa Ray

SLAUGHTER GANG I II III

RUTHLESS HEART I II III

By Willie Slaughter

FUK SHYT

By Blakk Diamond

DON'T F#CK WITH MY HEART I II

By Linnea

ADDICTED TO THE DRAMA I II III

IN THE ARM OF HIS BOSS II

By Jamila

YAYO I II III IV

A SHOOTER'S AMBITION I II

By S. Allen

Romell Tukes

TRAP GOD I II III

By Troublesome

FOREVER GANGSTA

GLOCKS ON SATIN SHEETS I II

By Adrian Dulan

TOE TAGZ I II III

LEVELS TO THIS SHYT

By Ah'Million

KINGPIN DREAMS I II

By Paper Boi Rari

CONFESSIONS OF A GANGSTA I II III

By Nicholas Lock

I'M NOTHING WITHOUT HIS LOVE

SINS OF A THUG

By Monet Dragun

CAUGHT UP IN THE LIFE I II III

By Robert Baptiste

NEW TO THE GAME I II III

MONEY, MURDER & MEMORIES I II

By **Malik D. Rice**

LIFE OF A SAVAGE I II III

A GANGSTA'S QUR'AN I II III

MURDA SEASON I II III

GANGLAND CARTEL I II III

CHI'RAQ GANGSTAS I II III

KILLERS ON ELM STREET

JACK BOYZ N DA BRONX

By **Romell Tukes**

LOYALTY AIN'T PROMISED I II

Jack Boyz N Da Bronx

By Keith Williams
QUIET MONEY I II III
THUG LIFE I II
EXTENDED CLIP I II
By **Trai'Quan**
THE STREETS MADE ME I II
By **Larry D. Wright**
THE ULTIMATE SACRIFICE I, II, III, IV, V, VI
KHADIFI
IF YOU CROSS ME ONCE
ANGEL I II
By **Anthony Fields**
THE LIFE OF A HOOD STAR
By Ca$h & Rashia Wilson
THE STREETS WILL NEVER CLOSE
By K'ajji
CREAM
By Yolanda Moore
NIGHTMARES OF A HUSTLA I II
By King Dream
CONCRETE KILLAZ
By Kingpen
HARD AND RUTHLESS
By Von Wiley Hall
GHOST MOB II
Stilloan Robinson
MOB TIES
By SayNoMore
BODYMORE MURDERLAND
By Delmont Player

Romell Tukes

FOR THE LOVE OF A BOSS
By C. D. Blue

Jack Boyz N Da Bronx

<u>BOOKS BY LDP'S CEO, CA$H</u>

Romell Tukes

CPSIA information can be obtained
at www.ICGtesting.com
Printed in the USA
LVHW010354300821
696398LV00007B/441